CACHE CAÑON

Other Five Star Westerns by Lauran Paine:

Tears of the Heart
Lockwood
The White Bird
The Grand Ones of San Ildefonso

CACHE CAÑON

A Western Story

LAURAN PAINE

Five Star
Unity, Maine

Five Star Western
Published in conjunction with Golden West Literary Agency.

February 1998

First Edition, Third Printing

Five Star Standard Print Western Series.

The text of this edition is unabridged.

Set in 11 pt. Plantin by Al Chase.

Printed in the United States on permanent paper.

Library of Congress Cataloging in Publication Data

Paine, Lauran.
    Cache Cañon : a western story / by Lauran Paine. — 1st ed.
      p.   cm.
    "Five star western"—T.p. verso.
    ISBN 0-7862-0989-5 (hc : alk. paper)
    I. Title.
PS3566.A34C24 1998
  813'.54—dc21
                                                       97-38422

CACHE CAÑON

Chapter One

THE FACTIONS OF CACHE VALLEY

There had been talk of the railroad coming through Rock City for several years. For obvious reasons the merchants kept the rumor alive. Rock City would grow and prosper. The "singing wires" were sure to follow. The telegraph, it was claimed, would put Rock City in touch with other towns and territories.

Embellishments to the anticipation included the establishment of a permanent Army installation. While soldiers were paid twelve dollars a month, enough of them would heighten Rock City's economy that for fifteen years had depended on the buffalo hunters and then drovers who had brought cattle onto thousands of virgin acres.

Rock City's economy had done moderately well after the stockmen found Cache Valley and had settled in. But Frank Terwilliger and his brother, Judah P., with six to eight hundred head of beef animals led the opposition because, if the railroad came, it would almost certainly lay track according to the route of least resistance, and that meant crossing through the Terwilliger brothers' vast land holdings. The brothers — hard, rawboned individuals — had driven slab-sided, wicked-horned Texas cattle into Cache Valley about the time buffalo hunters had decimated the native herds. They had prospered to the extent that they had built several ranch buildings and among other stockmen were highly respected. Neither Judah P. nor Frank Terwilliger had ever married. They actually had deed to six thousand acres, but Big T cattle ranged over not less than twenty thousand acres. No one had disputed their range rights, except for a handful of homesteaders, and they had been burned out or starved out. The Terwilligers remained in opposition even to the idea of a railroad.

George Crittenden, who owned the largest mercantile establishment in Rock City, favored the idea. Crittenden was a large, florid widower who was not above curtailing credit to the anti-railroad faction. He had come from "bloody" Kansas after the war where it was said there had been a price on his head for being a leader of the pro-slave Missourians who had participated in the sacking and burning of the Kansas town of Lawrence. True or not, too many years had passed. West of the Missouri River the war had been only of minimal concern, and afterward few made any effort to keep the conflict and its bitter animosities alive.

Rock City also did business through itinerant traveling men and the freight trade, which ensured high prices for just about everything. George Crittenden used this as the basis of his position favoring the railroad. Freight would be brought overland that would not only enhance the economy of the area but would also guarantee lower prices. He often used the price of a keg of horseshoes as an example. In areas where the railroad transported necessities at lower prices, a keg of horseshoes cost two dollars. In Rock City it cost four dollars. Sam Brennen, who ramrodded the stage company's corral yard, dryly told the saloonman's customers that he bought kegs of horseshoe blanks for a dollar and a half from free-hauling freighters, so Crittenden's profit had to be close to two dollars a keg. It was Crittenden's profiteering alone that explained why a keg cost more in Rock City than elsewhere.

Sam Brennen was a wiry, rawhide slip of a man, probably in his fifties. His corral yard had been a regular source of money for the local economy since about the time the Indians had been driven onto reservations. Sam was a dour individual who took his position as corral-yard boss seriously. Talk of the railroad was a direct threat to his livelihood.

The scrawny individual who owned and operated the Rock City hotel, Raymond Kemp, disliked the corral-yard boss who, he said, was a penny-pinching son-of-a-bitch, and mostly for that reason he favored the railroad. It meant his hotel business would increase, something he dearly needed and, if that was not his only reason for favoring the railroad, it was good enough.

Both factions had reason to be adamant, but with the passing of time and no clear evidence the railroad would come, other things that required and got foremost consideration took precedence, such as making a living in as isolated an area as Cache Valley. Railroad or no railroad, the area's economy depended in large part on cattle. Of the local cowmen the Terwilliger brothers had the largest holdings, which insured the respect they were given, especially by Rock City's merchants.

It was, however, on one of Sam Brennen's trips north to establish a way station that he encountered something that nearly stopped his heart. A company of surveyors were plotting the rugged uplands north of Cache Valley. It had always been assumed the railroad would follow the north-south road that had been established, as was the custom, following an old buffalo trail. Historically, buffalo took the line of least resistance. Road builders usually did the same.

The country north of Cache Valley was mountainous, rocky, heavily timbered, and had never been thoroughly explored for an excellent reason. The last hostile hold-outs had used this vast territory, and, while they eventually had been fought either to a standstill or forced to surrender in order not to be wiped out, stories still were rampant. Indian sightings as well as travelers seeing smoke rising on clear days from what had to be secret *rancherias* meant the soldiers had been unable to capture all the Indians who undoubtedly knew every nook and cranny of the darkly forbidding uplands and, being elusive by nature, were still up there.

Among those who believed this were the Terwilliger brothers who had lost cattle over the years, one or two at a time, and who with their riders had tracked their cattle and barefoot horses into the foothills before turning back. Among those foothills were a number of hidden valleys, some rather extensive, others no more than a few hundred yards deep. All of these places stopped where the high country commenced. A few bold individuals had entered these hidden valleys and found trails leading into the high country, but none had been bold enough to go farther. It was while passing along below one of those secret places that Sam Brennen had seen the surveyors. They were above a hidden valley among the piles of lava rock and huge, old, overripe firs and pines.

Sam completed his northward trip and returned with his light wagon low on its springs. Among the load were four kegs of horseshoes. He arrived at the corral yard at dusk, left the outfit to be off loaded outside the storeroom, and went directly to the saloon. He was hungry, too, but what he had seen took precedent.

The saloon proprietor's name was Cork Finney. His given name derived from emigrant parents who were from County Cork, Ireland. Evidently their homesickness for the "auld sod" went as far as having named the saloonman Cork. He was a bull-built man whose pale blue eyes missed little and who rarely drank. Whiskey was not his vice, but Cork Finney was rarely seen without a cigar.

As Cork Finney was putting the bottle and little glass in front of the corral-yard boss, he spoke around his cigar. He asked if Sam were ill. Getting a shake of the head after Brennen downed his whiskey, Cork Finney then said: "Something's bothering you."

And this time Brennen put a dark look across the bar and said: "There's surveyors up where the foothills begin. In that draw folks call Cache Cañon."

The saloonman raised his eyebrows. "In Cache Cañon?"

"No! Bold as brass on the bluff above."

"Why would anyone want to survey up there?"

Sam leaned and replied in a subdued voice: "*Railroad* surveyors."

Cork Finney regarded the older man. "Sam, that don't make sense. When the railroad comes, it'll follow the road. Was they atop the bluffs?"

"I already said they was."

"That's bad country, Sam. If they was up there, likely they crossed from north to south. They was in hostile country."

Sam Brennen refilled his little glass but did not raise it. Instead, he turned it, making a sticky, small circle.

Cork Finney relighted his dead cigar and trickled smoke as he said: "Maybe Charley ought to go up there."

Charley Bent was the constable, the only law for a hundred miles. He was large, capable, and well past his prime. When he visited the saloon for a nightcap, Cork Finney repeated what Sam Brennen had told him. Charley said that, if the hold-outs were up there, the last thing they'd want is the publicity that would follow a killing. Charley downed his nightcap, showing something less than the reaction of Sam and Cork. "If they're up there, they'd likely watch them surveyors until they was out of their territory."

Cork snorted. "*If* they're up there. Charley, you know as well as I do there's been too many sightings to believe they ain't up there."

Charley Bent's recent years had been moderately peaceful.

11

At his age he did not go out of his way to seek trouble, and for a fact it was a long ride, and surveyors had a right to do their work.

Even so, Cork Finney's saloon was not only a favorite watering hole for locals, it was also a clearing house for gossip, so it was inevitable that Sam Brennen's story got a wide circulation. Frank and Judah P. Terwilliger heard the story the next time they arrived in town for supplies. No one was more convinced there were Indians hiding in the wild, primitive uplands north of town than the Terwilliger brothers. Brennen's story made the brothers hunt down Brennen at the corral yard. He confirmed what the ranchers had heard, and, while Brennen would never have won a popularity contest, no one would deny Sam's reputation for being truthful.

The Terwilliger "boys" — both were in their sixties — left the corral yard to find the constable, who was at his jailhouse, savoring one of Finney's cigars. He listened to what the Terwilligers had to say and only showed an interest when Judah P. said he and his brother were going to take their riders and smoke out any tomahawks they could find.

Charley put the cigar aside and leaned forward on his desk. "You don't do any such thing. If they're up there, it's the Army's job. You ride up there . . . in the first place they'll see you coming before you even get close. I don't want no penny-ante war."

Judah P., a man of temper, restated his and his brother's intention to find those surveyors and Indians, too, if they could. The tomahawks had been stealing a critter or two for years, and, while this would not bankrupt the brothers, it was an irritant they intended to put a stop to.

Charley relighted his stogie, snapped the match, and fixed his gaze on Judah P. "It's the Army's business. You go up there and stir things up . . . Judah, for gosh sakes, leave it be.

Why would surveyors be up there?"

Frank spoke brusquely. "Railroad surveyors."

Charley frowned. "The railroad wouldn't go up there when they got the roadway to follow."

Judah P. said: "Why else would surveyors be up there?"

Charley did not even guess. "Take my word for it. If you ride up there loaded for bear, I'll stop you."

Judah P. jutted his jaw. "And do what?" he said.

Charley returned the other man's hostile stare. "Lock you up an' feed the key to a turkey. Boys, I mean it. Stay out of them uplands." His final words ended the discussion. "I'll send for the Army. It's their responsibility to hunt down hold-outs. I don't know a damned thing about any surveyors."

The Terwilligers had to be satisfied with that. They crossed over to George Crittenden's store and told the merchant the constable was going to get the Army to hunt down Indians while the Terwilligers hunted for railroad surveyors. There was no question about it, the Terwilligers were dead serious.

Crittenden had heard the story of the surveyors. His problem was believing railroad people would select the worst possible country for laying track. As a prominent member of the pro-railroad faction he wanted to believe the surveyors were plotting a route for the railroad that would follow the stage road. What the Terwilligers supposed didn't make any sense. Most folks who had heard about the surveyors shared the storekeeper's opinion that it was crazy to think track could be laid over and through the heavily forested uplands without great expense and a variety of difficulties that could be avoided by establishing a right-of-way either over the north-south road or close to it. That road had been pioneered by an assortment of early frontiersmen who never went over an obstacle if they could go around it. The road was clear all the way to the summit and part way down the other side. At the summit it went through a low notch where there was a broad, wide, mountain meadow. There were other such notches, but none went directly north and south.

For years, people using the north-south road had made camp at the mountain meadow where there was graze for animals and a busy, little, snow-water creek. The refuse and castoffs of dozens of travelers showed clearly that the summit meadow had been used for resting people and animals.

Both factions, the pro-railroaders and the opposition, speculated. Local opinion was unanimous in the conviction that the north-south road would be the best and easiest route for laying track. As the Terwilligers continued to spread the story, people still couldn't believe railroad surveyors would be in the highlands.

This mystery provoked some wild theories and wilder prognostications. The day after the Terwilliger brothers had braced Constable Charley Bent, Charley was in the saddle before dawn. He did not, however, go north. He rode west toward the shadow of the uplands. It was chilly, and Charley had tried to avoid saddlebacking the last few years. Between the cold and the long, westerly ride, Charley's mood was not cheerful.

Any way a man looked at it, this everlasting squabbling over the possibility of the railroad coming into Cache Valley was enough to drive a man to dipping snuff. His mood was not improved by what lay ahead and that was his intention to intercept the Terwilligers. It had occurred to him after the brothers had come to the jailhouse that the Terwilligers had either cooled down after their meeting at the jailhouse, or had decided that Charley hadn't been bluffing when he had told them in no uncertain terms what he would do if they persisted in their talk about going tomahawk hunting. There was a possibility that his ride to make an interception would result in nothing. This thought added to his irritation.

14

By the time the sun was climbing, most of the predawn chill had dissipated, and by that time Charley was miles westerly in approximately the area where the Terwilligers would appear with their riders, if they appeared. When he shed his range-man's coat and was securing it behind the cantle, his horse raised its head with little ears pointing southward.

Charley saw them coming at a slow lope and looked around for concealment. He was about a mile south of the timber country and had to settle for a ragged jumble of prehistoric rocks. Visibility was excellent, but, while he could see the riders, they were too distant for him to identify individually. That only mattered for a short period of time. From his boulder hide-out he eventually recognized Judah P. in the lead. He didn't look for Frank. Instead, he counted the horsemen, and, while the Terwilligers kept four or five riders from spring to fall, Charley's count — he made it three times — came up with the number twelve. He figured the Terwilligers' prominence had encouraged other stockmen to join in the proposed manhunt. Their argument would be that the Terwilligers weren't the only cowmen who had been raided over the years.

Charley waited until the riders hauled down to a steady walk before riding out of the rocks and stopping directly in their path. Their reaction to seeing Constable Bent was to slacken their gait more and to speak among themselves.

Judah P. called to his brother, and the pair of them left their companions and loped in Charley's direction.

As far as the grizzled old lawman was concerned, he had stopped the horsemen. Because he was the only recognized law, they knew he wouldn't just palaver with the Terwilligers. Before he rode back the way he had come, he would have laid down the law to every jack-man his unexpected presence had thrown into confusion.

Chapter Two

STRANGERS AND RUMORS

Frank Terwilliger was the calmer of the brothers. Where they met the constable, Frank only nodded. His brother was different. He had a quick temper, and under these circumstances he was less rattled at Charley Bent's appearance than he was ready to argue.

Facing them in the saddle, Charley said: "I told you, if you go up there, making trouble, I'll lock you up."

Judah P. reddened. "We're out lookin' for cattle."

Charley gazed at the other man and said dryly: "Sure you are. Twelve of you armed to the gills, headin' for Cache Cañon an' the trail leadin' up. Judah, you 'n' your riders go home."

Frank spoke for the first time. "Did you send for the Army?"

Charley hadn't. Next to long horseback rides, he hated writing letters. "Not yet," he replied.

Judah P. snorted: "Don't bother. We'll do their job for 'em."

"Not today you won't. Frank . . . ?"

"We got to do it. The fellers with us all lost cattle. Charley, waitin' for the Army'll likely take months. Us fellers have had enough. We should've done this years ago."

The horsemen farther back were getting restless. One of them yelled to the Terwilligers. "Take him along."

That idea kept the brothers quiet for a while before Frank began calmly: "Charley . . . ?"

The constable's mood was not alleviated by this suggestion. Looking straight at Judah P., he interrupted: "Nobody's goin'

16

up there. Not today nor any other time. Now get back the way you come. Judah, you ride back with me."

"Why?"

"Because I'm goin' to lock you up."

"No sir! Not on your life." Judah P. yanked loose the tie-down thong over his holstered Colt.

Charley did not move. Frank Terwilliger growled at his brother. "Leave it be, Judah. There'll be another time."

Frank's influence over his brother had always been strong. It was this time, too, for while Judah P. remained tense enough to fight, indecision troubled him. Charley had no intention of fighting. Not against twelve of them. He softened his voice when he offered a compromise. "Judah, I won't take you in if you ride back with the others."

Frank addressed his brother. "That's fair enough," and reined back toward the waiting men, leaving Judah and Charley regarding each other.

Charley spoke quietly again. "It's not worth us fightin' over."

Judah reined around without a word and went back to join his brother and the others. Charley let go a sigh of relief, waited until he saw the party of stockmen riding back the way they had come, then he, too, turned to follow his own trail back. Without the benefit of a companion he told his horse that it had been a close call. He knew, if Frank hadn't been along, it might have ended differently because Charley couldn't have backed down. Today, if he'd heard the rumor in Rock City, he might have agreed with it. It was said he was too old for the job. He knew some folks were in favor of replacing him with a younger man.

By the time he had the town in sight it was dark. Charley put up his horse, forked a generous flake of hay to it, and went to the jailhouse where, after lighting a lamp and pushing his hat back, he sat at the desk. *Maybe I am too old*. For a fact that ride out there and back had wearied the hell out of him.

He visited Cork Finney's Pleasure Palace where he was greeted in a subdued way by the other patrons. Even Cork would not look Charley in the eye until he had downed a nightcap. Then Cork said: "Folks saw you ride out before sunrise." Cork waited for a reply, but Charley only smiled, put a coin beside his little glass, and returned to the street.

Night had set in. Charley had no trouble trudging up to his room at the hotel and would have bedded down, but the proprietor, Raymond Kemp, caught him in the dingy hallway and said he'd seen Charley leave town before sunup. Again, Charley did not take the bait. He simply said: "It's been a long day, Ray. Good night."

Two days later, again in the Pleasure Palace, Charley met a cowman named Daniels, one of the party that had ridden with the Terwilliger brothers. Daniels said: "Frank wasn't mad, but you should have seen Judah P. when he caught up with us. He was mad enough to chew bullets and spit rust."

Daniels always smiled a lot. But even his smile could not disguise the fact that he was uncomfortable in Charley's presence. Shortly before they parted, Daniels said: "Maybe we was wrong. Frank told us you'd sent for the Army, but you got to understand we been losing cattle for years."

For this admission Charley bought Daniels a drink and gave him a light pat on the back. Then Daniels left the saloon.

Cork Finney had heard the brief conversation and offered Charley a drink on the house. When the constable accepted and had downed the whiskey, Cork asked him a question. "There's talk that, when you rode out the other day, you went up to the badlands lookin' for Indians. Is it true?"

Charley leaned on the bar, wearing a smile. "What Indians, Cork?"

"You know. Them hold-outs up there."

"Have you ever seen one, Cork?"

Cork reddened. "I never been up there because folks say they'll kill anyone that looks like he's huntin' 'em."

Charley's reply was short. "I've never seen one, an' I've ridden up there."

"You don't believe it, Charley? Hell, everyone in town an' out among the cattlemen believe it. Folks have even said. . . ."

"Cork, folks say a lot of things that are pure bull."

After the constable left, a range man who had overheard the conversation came over to the bar, ordered a jolt, and commented: "Them hold-outs been stealin' a cow now an' then sure as I'm standin' here. Maybe the constable's blind or is an Injun lover."

Cork was irritated by the range man's attitude as well as by what he'd said. He pulled the rag he habitually wore tucked into his breeches and used it to dry his hands, which were not wet. "Charley Bent's the best law man around, an' if he believes there's no tomahawks hidin' in the mountains, that's good enough for me."

The range man lost his smile, put a coin beside his empty jolt glass, and left. Cork watched the spindle doors wag back and forth behind the rider and frowned. What he'd told the range man about Charley Bent was true, but the rest of what he'd said bothered him a little. Like the majority of townsmen, he was at least half convinced there were hold-outs in the badlands.

In a town no larger than Rock City any stranger who wasn't just passing through was a novelty. The afternoon, southbound stage brought four strangers to Rock City. One of them had a

neatly trimmed beard, wore a curly brimmed derby hat, pants, and coat that matched. At the saloon he asked Cork if he knew where he could find a man named Alexander Morton. Cork explained how to get to Lex's place and watched the stranger leave. *What,* he wondered, *would that greenhorn, city man want to see old Lex for?* Morton, a one-legged ex-Confederate, pretty much stayed to himself. If he bathed or had his hair cut, it was not often.

The other three strangers were rough-looking men, large and muscular. They went first to the hotel to hire rooms, then went to the café. They did not visit Cork's place. They hung around town three days, and they visited George Crittenden at the Emporium. Otherwise, they kept to themselves.

On the fourth day the town blacksmith, a short, massive man named Andrew Jackson Buck, came to the jailhouse. He wanted to know if Charley had seen the strangers. Charley had. He'd seen dozens of strangers over the years, peddlers, relatives of someone, one time even a snake-oil peddler, and an itinerant dentist who had pulled a number of teeth before moving on to the next town.

Buck wore a solemn expression when he asked if Charley had talked to the strangers and got a negative wag of the head.

"Why? Do you know them?" asked Charley.

"One of 'em," said the blacksmith. "In those days his name was Morgan. I asked Ray Kemp at the hotel if the strangers had signed the register. They had, an' Ray showed me the ledger. Them strangers was registered as Bill Smith, Al Shokely, an' Ben Leathergood."

Charley shifted in his chair. Normally he was a patient man, but now he was getting impatient. "Andy, you're takin' a long time to get it out."

Buck cleared his throat before saying: "Eight years ago down at Brownsville I was with the posse that went after a bank

robber. We didn't catch him. In fact, we never even saw him. But I was in the bank when he robbed it."

Charley leaned forward. "Which one?"

"The one callin' himself Bill Smith, an' I was as close to him inside the bank as I am to you. I'll never forget his face, except now he's got a beard."

Charley leaned back, eyeing the blacksmith who was known to be cranky at times. Although he had an irritable disposition, there was nothing wrong with either his eyesight or his memory.

As Buck hoisted himself up, he offered some advice. "Be careful, Constable."

Charley nodded, waited until the blacksmith was gone, then reset his hat and went outside. There was no sign of the strangers. It was possible they could be inside any of the establishments. He crossed to the Emporium. Because he had known George Crittenden a long time, he was mildly surprised at the merchant's answers to his questions about the strangers.

Crittenden said: "They been in the store, but that's about all I can tell you."

Charley persisted, and Crittenden got increasingly evasive.

When Charley asked if the strangers had bought anything, Crittenden said: "Tobacco is all."

The constable left the store, feeling that George Crittenden was involved with the strangers somehow and knew more than he was saying.

He finally located the strangers in Jed Ames's harness shop. When the constable entered, they eyed him from blank faces. The harness maker winked at Charley. He had pegged the strangers as city men. They didn't wear neckties, but otherwise each man wore matching breeches and coats. Also, each man wore a holstered six-gun.

Ames introduced Charley. The strangers nodded without offering their names or a handshake. They left the shop together, which made Jed Ames comment that every time he'd seen them, they had been together. Charley's impression was that the strangers had business in Rock City, but exactly what that business was had never been stated, otherwise by now it would have been common knowledge. When Charley left after visiting with the harness maker for a time, he saw the strangers, sitting on a bench outside the gunsmith's shop, like crows on a fence. Likewise, they also saw Charley and watched him go down the street.

Charley entered the jailhouse. Inside, he dropped his hat on the desk, went to the solitary, barred, front window, and looked northward. They were still up there on the bench.

To Charley's knowledge, they had broken no law in his district. He wondered if Andy Buck could be mistaken. The only way he was going to know that was to visit the smithy and convince Andy Buck to walk up the duck boards on the opposite side of the street as far as the harness shop and take another good look at Smith and make a positive identification that he was, indeed, Morgan, the bank robber.

When Charley walked into the smithy, Buck was sweating a tire onto an old wagon wheel. He listened irritably to Charley, straightened up, and said: "Right now? I got the rim at the right temperature for the wheel."

"Andy, he's not goin' to sit there all day."

Buck wiped both hands on a dirty towel and left the smithy. Charley watched him cross the street and walk northward. It hadn't occurred to him that the bank robber might recognize the blacksmith.

His anxiety evaporated when the blacksmith returned. He hadn't gone the full northward distance. As he frowned at his cooling rim, he said: "There ain't no way around it, Charley. That feller is Morgan. I admit he was clean shaven in Brownsville, but like I told you, I'd know him anywhere."

Charley walked northward, too, but on the same side of the street. They were still sitting up there, and the bank robber was smoking a cigar. As Charley avoided people going to the Emporium, he watched the strangers. They spoke among themselves and were not aware of the constable's approach until he stopped and said: "It's a good town, if you gents are interested. For miles in three directions it's as good a range country as you'll find."

The man now calling himself Bill Smith removed the cigar, eyed Charley and the badge he wore, and remarked: "Looks to me like most of the land's been taken up."

Charley did not know whether they had ridden out to look around or not. He would have to ask Jim Neely, the liveryman. Meanwhile, he kept the conversation alive. "There's open range. It's a long way out, but it's got grass and water."

The stranger who was more thickly built than his companions spoke. "For a fact, it's a nice town. You got many old-timers around?"

There were some. Each spring there were fewer.

The thickly built man spoke again. "Best way to know about a countryside is to talk to them as been around a long time."

Charley agreed with that. "There's an old gaffer named Morton, Lex Morton. He's been here since the days of the buffler hunters. Got a wooden leg. He lives in a shack behind Doc Reese's place. You can't miss it. Old Lex found a bucket of red paint somewhere an' painted his front door red. If you visit him, take along a bottle, an' he'll talk your leg off."

"Is that what happened to him?" they joked, and then thanked the constable. Shortly after he had crossed the street in the direction of the jailhouse, the three strangers went among the shacks, looking for a red door. They found it.

It was impossible not to.

Charley went to the café, ate, returned to the street, and leaned against an upright in the shade. He did not see the strangers, so he walked over to the jailhouse, sat down, propped his feet atop the desk, and smiled at the gun rack across the room. He had laid a trap and would now wait.

It was late afternoon before his visitor tapped timidly on the door, walked in hat in hand, and waited until Charley nodded toward a chair before sitting down. If the strangers had primed the old man, he gave no sign of it. Having lived into his ripe years, he'd developed resistance. He'd also developed the capability many old men had of not showing their liquor. He eased into a chair, his wooden leg extended.

Charley leaned on his desk as he said: "What did you tell 'em, Lex?"

"Tell who?"

"Them three strangers. I told 'em, if anyone knew this country, it would be you."

The old man shifted his wooden leg and relaxed. It had been a long time since anyone had complimented him. "I told 'em what they wanted to know. They was interested in the north country, up around the badlands."

"Did they say why, Lex?"

"They're surveyors."

Charley eased back in his chair. Sam Brennen's story was true. "What are they surveying, Lex?"

"I got no idea. All they said was that they was surveyors. When I asked what they was surveyin', they got to asking about other things." The old man paused to wipe his running nose with the cuff of his ancient coat. "Want to know what I think, Constable?"

Charley nodded.

"I think they're lookin' for that cache folks say was buried

24

up there about thirty years ago."

Charley smiled.

The old man did, too, as he said: "Everybody an' his uncle has searched for that. I tell you, Constable, if there ever was a cache, by now it's been found. Me, I don't believe there ever was one. Every place has a story of a hidden cache. It's what a friend of mine, dead now twenty years, called a myth."

Charley avoided agreeing or disagreeing. "The old-timers named the countryside Cache Valley, an' there's that wide draw up there that's named Cache Cañon."

The old man gazed steadily at the constable. "Years back I scouted for the Army around a settlement called Bountiful, an' it was a damned desert."

Charley handed the old man a silver cartwheel.

He considered it for a long time before saying: "You don't have to pay me, Constable."

Charley's reply was that he hadn't given the old man the cartwheel for his information. He had given it to him for not saying a word about the strangers' visit to anyone else.

After Lex Morton left, Charley cocked his chair back, clasped both hands behind his head, and this time, when he stared at the gun rack, he did not smile.

With dusk settling, the constable went up to the corral yard where Sam Brennen was bawling out a red-headed whip twice his size. When he saw Charley, he growled one last time and left the huge stage driver standing like he'd taken root.

They went to Brennen's cluttered, little office where Charley was offered a drink. He declined, but Brennen upended the bottle, coughed, wiped his mouth, and pointed to a chair that had been wired to hold it together. Charley sat gingerly as Brennen said: "That damned big oaf. If I could replace him,

25

I'd fire his butt tomorrow."

"What did he do?"

"Stopped to let a passenger get out to pee, an' drove off without him."

Charley said: "Sam, tell me about them surveyors you saw up yonder. Where exactly was they?"

"On that high rim above Cache Cañon. Sure as I'm settin' here, they work for the railroad."

"Would you recognize 'em if you saw 'em?"

Brennen scowled. "I'd've needed a telescope. They was up there, an' I was passin' the cañon with my wagon." Brennen snorted. "A keg of horseshoes for four dollars. I get 'em for a dollar an' a half. George Crittenden's a damned robber."

Charley sighed. Sam Brennen was a cantankerous individual if there ever was one, and he had been no help at all.

Over at the saloon Charley saw the three strangers, sitting at a small table topped with jolt glasses and a bottle. Only one nodded, the bearded man named Smith.

Cork got out a jolt glass and filled it before the constable reached the bar. After Charley had tossed it off, Cork said: "You see them fellers over at the table?"

Charley nodded and turned the jolt glass upside down before Cork could refill it. "What about 'em?" he asked.

"There's talk around town that they are fugitive outlaws."

Charley smiled. "Fugitive outlaws don't stay in one place a week. They move an' keep movin'."

Cork scowled. "Well, who are they? What business they got in Rock City?"

"They're surveyors, Cork."

The saloonman's eyes narrowed. "Are they now? Only reason for surveyors bein' in this country is to map out the route for a railroad."

26

Chapter Three

SOME SURPRISES

Judah P. arrived in town a couple of hours after sunrise. He entered the jailhouse, glaring. Charley sighed. Judah P. did not take a chair. He stood in front of the desk. "Frank an' me want to know what's goin' on!"

Charley eyed the angry man. "What do you mean, what's goin' on?"

"Them three fellers, ridin' over our north range. We don't like trespassin'."

Charley leaned forward on the desk. "What three men?"

"One's got a beard. The others shave. One of our riders was up north, lookin' for a bull we ain't seen in a couple of weeks. He told us, when he caught up with 'em, that they opined how they was from town and lookin' the country over. Frank thinks they're rustlers, sure as hell. We never did find the bull."

"They got rooms at the hotel, Judah. They're surveyors."

Judah P.'s agitation increased. "Railroaders! I knew it. I told Frank they was studyin' the north country for a railroad."

Charley ignored the rawboned, tall man's agitated condition. "They been here a week or more, Judah. I got no idea why."

"Now you know, Charley. If we catch 'em on our range again . . . !"

"Judah, I told you once before. If I have to, I'll lock you up."

The tall man snorted. "For what? Protectin' our range?"

Charley sighed and leaned back away from the desk, gazing stonily at Terwilliger. "If they do somethin' against the law, I'll go after 'em. That's my job. Your job is not to make trouble."

Judah P. went to the door and, with one hand on the latch, made his final statement before leaving. "You ain't doin' much of a job if you don't keep trespassers off our range."

Charley spent an hour writing and rewriting two missives. The one was a letter to the authorities down in Brownsville. The other was a letter to an Army officer he'd known for years. He went across the street to the post office in the Emporium and mailed the two letters. Then he went to the smithy where he was greeted by Andy Buck with a wary: "Good mornin'."

The purpose of Charley's visit was to verify again the identity of the stranger named Smith. Andy Buck was annoyed. "I told you, I don't forget a face, an', when I saw that outlaw son-of-a-bitch, it liked to scairt the whey out of me. He's Morgan, Constable, sure as I'm standin' here. Are you goin' to lock him up?"

Charley knew the blacksmith would not like his reply, but he said it anyway. "Not unless he breaks the law. I sent an inquiry down to Brownsville. If they answer good enough to satisfy me that you're right, I'll lock him up."

"On what charge? Brownsville's in Texas, not Colorado."

"Extradition, Andy. I can lock him up and send him down to Brownsville."

The blacksmith wasn't satisfied. "If word gets around I told you who he is, I'll get a bullet in the back."

"Only you 'n' me know what you told me, an' that's the way it's goin' to be."

As the constable was turning to leave, Andy Buck told him: "Judah was in town today. Did you see him? He told me them three strangers was seen up north near the foothills, trespassin' on Terwilliger land."

"He came to the jailhouse, Andy, an' told me about the strangers bein' up there."

"Well, then, can't you arrest 'em for trespassin'?"

Charley's patience was wearing thin. "Andy, this is open-range country. Strangers wouldn't know they was trespassin'. Nobody builds fences."

It was a beautiful day. The air was as clear as glass, and without a cloud in the sky it would be warm later on. Charley returned to the jailhouse unmindful of these blandishments. Until he received an answer to his letter to Brownsville, he could not act, but, meanwhile, the strangers were taking up a goodly portion of his time. He'd been warned against outlaws before, and out of all the warnings none had proven to be true. But Charley was a patient man. In cases like this, he had also to be careful and do nothing until he had proof one way or the other.

In the early afternoon Lex Morton met Charley while he was making a round. It was outside the harness shop where there was a bench. Morton sat down as he said: "Judah P. was in town this mornin'."

Charley nodded a little absently. "We had a talk."

"What about?" Morton asked, and Charley put an annoyed look at the old man without replying.

Morton shifted on the bench. His wooden leg always had to be shoved straight out. There was no hinge at the knee. He had an ingrained habit of shrinking into himself when uncomfortable, which he did now. " 'Scuse me for askin'."

Charley relented to the extent that he joined Morton on the bench. "Them strangers was ridin' over Terwilliger range. One of the Terwilliger riders come onto them, told Judah P., an' he was real upset when he visited me this mornin'."

"It don't take much to upset Judah P.," Morton said dryly. "My brother come down from Laramie a while back. He works for the law there. He heard about a grisly murder up Montana way. He believes he's seen the feller who did it in Laramie. And something about that husky stranger reminds me of the no-good he described. Leastwise, the feller my brother suspicioned ain't around Laramie no more. He might have headed south."

Charley leaned back, squinting across the street in the direction of Cork Finney's Pleasure Palace. "You can't tell much from a description, Lex."

Morton shook his head. "I know that. I've just got a feeling, Constable."

"You haven't said anything to anybody else, have you?"

"Constable, the last time I spoke up, instead of listening, a damned Yankee shot me in the leg. Since them days I learnt to keep my mouth shut, even with my brother."

Charley returned to the jailhouse. He now had two townsmen who thought they could identify a pair of the strangers as outlaws, but whether Lex Morton, who was by nature a diffident individual, could actually be trusted in this case was a highly questionable matter.

For now all Charley could do was await a response to his Brownsville letter. Fortunately he had the patience. He hadn't lived to nearly sixty without learning a few things, and of those fifty-plus years he had been a lawman for twenty-five years. The law never hurried.

He went up to the hotel and was told by Ray Kemp that the three strangers had not returned from wherever they'd gone the previous night, but that some of their property was still in their rooms. Charley returned to the jailhouse to ponder. If the strangers had not returned since the day before, there most likely had to be a good reason.

There was. By late afternoon both the Terwilligers came to the jailhouse to tell Charley that another of their riders at the upcountry line shack had found the fresh tracks of three horses. He hadn't heard a thing, nor had his horse nickered, which meant, according to the Terwilligers, that the unknown horsemen knew the line shack was there and had stayed clear. Their range man had told the Terwilligers he had followed the sign until he had reached the foothills before turning back. The tracks led into that wide draw called Cache Cañon.

Judah P. proposed that the strangers had likely used the old trail up out of the cañon to reach the highlands.

Charley frowned. "Why in hell would they go up there?"

Frank replied: "They're greenhorns. I'd guess they don't know about the Indians."

Charley assured the Terwilligers he'd look into the matter, and they left.

The constable would have to ride his butt sore to get up where those strangers went. He speculated on whether they would attempt night riding and came to the conclusion that, since they knew there might be a Terwilliger rider up there such as the one they had met, they probably would avoid a similar experience precisely by riding at night. The more he thought about that, the more he was willing to accept it. But that was not his problem. *Why would those strangers go up there at all?*

Charley could hardly reach the foothills before dusk set in. He went up to the saloon for a beer. Cork Finney considered his expression and asked what was wrong. The answer — "Nothing." — did not satisfy him, but he understood why it had been given, so he went up the bar where a tub of oily water was half filled with used glasses and went to work, rinsing and drying.

While he was doing this, Sam Brennen came in, looked

31

around, and took a place beside the constable. He kept his voice low when he said he had just received word that the southbound stage had been held up early that morning. He also said the whip had seen two of the road agents in some rocks while the third one stopped his coach and robbed the passengers and the driver. Sam, being a fidgety, nervous individual, was irritated by Charley's silence as he spoke. "Constable, where they stopped the stage is near that Point of the Rocks. It'd ought to be easy to find their trail."

Charley nodded. "Four years ago another stage was stopped there."

Brennen nodded. "That's the place. There hasn't been a stage stopped since then. Are you goin' up there?"

"In the morning, Sam. It'd be dark if I left now."

Brennen called to Cork for a drink, and, when the bottle and glass came, he filled his glass but not Charley's.

After Brennen left, Cork came down the bar, drying his hands. "Charley, them three? Sam said two was in the rocks and the other one stopped the stage."

Charley nodded. "I heard him. I'll go up there in the morning."

It was a little shy of sunrise when Charley left Rock City. He reached what was called Point of the Rocks with a climbing sun outlining every detail. The outlaws had ridden west. He followed the sign until it veered to the north. If he went on, as sure as hell was hot they would see him. In open country movement was noticeable. He turned back and reached town in the afternoon. Sam Brennen saw him ride by and followed all the way to the livery barn where Charley kept his horse.

Sam was excited. "Did you find 'em?"

Charley led his horse out back to the trough with Sam accompanying him. He asked the same question again, and the constable, holding his horse on a loose rope, replied: "I know where they went. After stoppin' your stage, they went northwest into the foothills."

"Where'd they go from there?"

Charley said he had turned back, and Sam got angry. "What in hell does the town council pay you for, Charley?"

"Well, for one thing, not to hit someone when they say what you just did."

When Brennen left the barn, Charley turned his horse into an empty stall and forked in some feed before heading for the jailhouse.

He was trying to fit bits and pieces together when Jed Ames walked in without his wax-stiffened apron. He sat down, shoved his legs out, and said: "I heard about the stage bein' stopped. Charley, if you figure to trail 'em, I'll volunteer to ride along."

Charley's answer was given thoughtfully. He just might need Ames with him if he went through Cache Cañon and up the trail to the highlands. There was only one good trail up to the primitive area, and it was through Cache Cañon. The strangers had gone up there. He was sure of that. He thanked the harness maker, saying Jed would be the first man he'd call if it came to that.

Ames was not quite finished. "Sam said there was three of them."

"I know what you're thinkin', Jed, but many times there've been five or six men have stopped stages."

Ames did not give up easily. "Did you know them three strangers was gone all night?"

"I knew it. There's got to be somethin' better than that, Jed. You can't lock folks up for stayin' out all night."

The harness maker arose. "Let me know when you want to ride," he said, and left the jailhouse.

The following day he went down to the smithy where for

once Buck wasn't busy. The blacksmith offered Charley hot coffee which the constable declined, not because he had anything against coffee, but because the blacksmith boiled and reboiled the stuff until it was strong enough to float horseshoes. He asked Andy when he'd left Brownsville and got an immediate response.

"Some time back, about a day or two after the bank was robbed."

"Did the law down there ask you to identify the robber?"

"No, the sheriff gathered a posse and went to find him. After he got back, I saddled up to leave. The sheriff didn't catch Morgan with that posse, and I didn't figure to set around until he caught him."

Charley exhaled a long breath and turned to leave.

The blacksmith stopped him with a question. "You ain't told anyone, have you?"

"I said I wouldn't, Andy."

On that point Buck seemed satisfied, but he had another question. "I heard at the café them fellers was gone out of town for a spell. Charley, there's somethin' goin' on, ain't there?"

The older man answered with a nod before saying: "That's what bothers me."

"Lock up that one I identified for you and kick the truth out of him."

Charley nodded and left. Between the blacksmith and the harness maker there was a lack of understanding that Charley had to follow the law. His personal opinion was that there was no comparison between justice and the law, but he was sworn to uphold the law, which meant his personal feelings did not matter.

Ray Kemp could be unmistakably identified by the way he walked. No one else in the countryside had such a loping gait. He appeared to be always in a hurry. It was no different today when he entered the jailhouse. He tossed something onto the constable's desk. Charley smoothed the crumpled scrap of paper out and read it while Kemp shifted into a chair.

When Charley looked up, Kemp said: "Found it when I was cleaning out one of their rooms."

Charley considered the paper again. "Did you show this to anyone, Ray?"

"Not a soul, except you. Charley, ain't that one of them three strangers?"

The constable leaned back. "Sure fits the description. I don't recollect his name."

"Shokely," Kemp replied. "What kind of a son-of-a-bitch does something like that?"

Charley didn't answer. He was seeking the date on the scrap from a newspaper. On the particular page on his desk there was no date.

"Charley, I've known some of them, highwaymen, hold-up men, whiskey peddlers on the reservations, but, by Gawd, I never knew one that'd do that."

Charley only half heard. For the third time he read of a solitary outlaw who had shot a man, his wife, and seven-year-old daughter. The article offered no opinion why it had been done, only the outrage even a supposedly neutral reporter had felt. Charley asked about the rest of the newspaper.

Kemp got uncomfortable when he answered. "I hate cleanin' up after men like that. Fact is, I burnt some of the trash they left in their rooms. I'd've burnt that, too, except the black headline got my attention. Charley, can't you lock Shokely up?"

"For what? The description fits, but hell, Ray, we don't even know when or where this happened." Charley leaned forward. "How many men do you know who would fit this description?"

Kemp nodded. Unlike Sam Brennen, he did not get mad, but he said: "One of them three was carryin' that piece of newspaper. It'd be Shokely. Anyway, I found it in his room. Can you lock him up on suspicion until you find out more?"

Charley explained why he couldn't just walk up to Al Shokely and arrest him. "The paper wouldn't hold up when the circuit-ridin' judge got here, an', if Shokely was turned loose, which he sure as hell would be, he'd disappear."

Charley then did something he usually avoided. He mentioned that another of the three strangers could be a bank robber, and the hotelman showed no surprise. He was scrawny and unwashed, but there was nothing wrong with his mind. He said: "That'd most likely mean all three of them is wanted men, wouldn't it?"

Charley agreed. He was beginning to be frustrated by the constraints of the law.

Kemp made a suggestion. "Maybe if you wrote copies of that article and sent it around . . . ?"

Charley, who hated writing letters, replied: "I'd have to write to all the states west of the Missouri, an' sure as hell the one I missed would be where this happened, *if* all the lawmen I wrote answered."

Kemp asked: "What are you goin' to do?"

"First off, I'd take it as a favor, if you didn't tell a soul about this. In the meantime, I'm goin' to try 'n' figure some way to find out why they're here."

Kemp boosted himself out of the chair as he said: "Any way I can help? Don't worry about me mentionin' anythin'."

Following Kemp's departure, Charley minutely studied the paper, but there was nothing in the article that helped. Out of frustration he went up to Finney's saloon. Both the Terwilligers were there, and Judah P. in particular appeared to have already

36

had a couple of jolts from the bottle in front of them on the bar.

Cork was made nervous by Charley's arrival. He knew the Terwilligers and Charley Bent well enough to know one spark would start a fight, and, while he would favor the marshal if it came to that, he also had what was to him a fortune invested in the back-bar mirror and shelves of bottles. He leaned forward as he set up the jolt glass in front of Charley and whispered: "Don't get Judah fired up."

Charley had deliberately taken a place at the bar distant from the cowmen. If he had known they were in the saloon, he would not have entered. He watched as Cork, who kept an ash wagon-spoke and a sawed-off shotgun on the shelf below the bar, got more nervous by the minute. If there was anything good about this, it had to be that Charley and the Terwilligers were Cork's only customers, but that could change at any moment.

Judah P. considered his empty glass and growled at Cork for a refill. While Cork was refilling the little glass, Judah P. slowly turned to glare at the lawman.

His brother warned: "Leave it be."

Judah P. continued to stare.

Charley put a coin beside his empty glass, an obvious indication to the others that he meant to leave. Before he could step away from the bar, Judah P. said: "Gawd damn' Injun lover." No sooner were the words out of his mouth than he got a sharp jab from his brother, which he ignored.

Charley acted deaf, turned from the bar, and crossed about half the distance to the doors when Judah P. spoke again, this time in a louder tone of voice.

"Maybe them cattle that's been missin' among us stockmen ain't all been stole by hold-outs."

Charley turned slowly. "What does that mean?"

Judah P. did not hesitate to reply. "It means maybe, since you never done anythin' about our losses. . . ."

This time Frank's jab was harder. Frank had meant for it to be. But the whiskey his brother had taken on seemed to aggravate his natural bad temper. He winced but finished what he'd meant to say, and did not even look at Frank. "Maybe it wasn't the Injuns. Maybe it was the law."

Charley walked slowly back toward Judah P. until he was just within reach, then he hit him so hard on the jaw that the tall man dropped to the floor.

Frank had his hand on his six-gun when Cork struck him with the wagon-spoke. Frank doubled over in pain.

Charley took both their sidearms and told Cork to advise them that, when they felt better, they could get the guns at the jailhouse. He turned again to leave, and this time there was no interruption to his progress through the doors.

Chapter Four

CHARLEY'S PROBLEMS

A day later it bothered Charley when Ray Kemp hitched his way to a chair, sat down, and, looking straight at him, said: "They're gone." There was no need to explain who he meant. Before Charley could speak, Kemp added: "Last night, an', by Gawd I'm goin' to lock the front door. They owed me six dollars."

"How do you know they're gone?" the constable asked and got a glare.

"Because all their personal things are gone."

Charley stood up, a sign their meeting was over. Kemp also arose slowly, still thinking about his six dollars.

Charley went down to the livery barn where Jim Neely told him the three saddle animals the strangers had hired were still out. "I hope them fellers take care. They got three of my best horses." He cocked his head a little. "Is there somethin' wrong, Constable? They didn't run off with my horses, did they?"

When Charley answered, he did not mention his misgivings. "They'd know to take care of your horses."

That didn't answer Neely's question, so the liveryman asked another. "Where do they go, doin' all that saddlebackin'?"

Charley's reply was truthful. "I don't know where they go, but I'd give a month's pay to find out."

After the constable left, Neely really began to worry. Why would the constable ask about his horses unless he knew something? Bothered by Charley's visit, Neely went over to the smithy. Andy Buck was in the process of being paid for shoeing an animal by a large man with eyes darker than midnight. Together, Neely and Buck watched the large man lead his twelve-hundred-pound animal outside, finger the cinch, swing up, and ride north through town.

Andy's customary crankiness had been ameliorated by what he had put in his pocket. He smiled at Neely who neglected to smile back. "The constable was at the barn, askin' about them three strangers I let out horses to."

Andy's smile faded. "Why?"

"He didn't say. You know how close-mouthed he can be."

"Did he tell you anythin' about the strangers?"

Neely hesitated before replying. "Not that I recollect. No."

"Did he mention me, or somethin' like that?"

"No."

Buck let go a sigh of relief. Ever since he had told Charley about the bank robber now calling himself Smith, he had developed a feeling that it would be unwise to stand with his back exposed. He now wished the constable would do something about it — like arresting him.

Neely went back across the street and was about to enter the runway of his stable when he saw one of Sam Brennen's stages make the wide sashay to avoid hitting either of the log walls with a wheel. He paused, remembering that one of Sam's stages had been robbed. In his present frame of mind he had no difficulty connecting the act with the three strangers. What next attracted his attention was George Crittenden who was bringing in his top buggy with the red running gear and yellow wheels. He then forgot about the constable and the strangers.

At the same time at the jailhouse, Charley was facing the Terwilliger brothers, now recovered from their encounter with the constable on the night before. Frank did the talking. Judah P., his jaw slightly discolored, was silent. Frank wanted their guns back.

40

Charley put them both, butt first, atop the desk. As Frank approached the desk to pick up the weapons, the constable addressed Judah P. "I expect you'd been drinkin' yesterday. Judah, you're old enough to know what happens when someone loses their temper."

He got no reply. Frank had probably told his brother not so much as to say good morning to Charley Bent. For men so different in many ways, Judah P.'s opinion of his brother had always been high. He gazed sullenly at the constable as though he'd lost his tongue. The only word he uttered was when Frank handed Judah P. his six-gun: "Thanks." He holstered his Colt, and moved toward the door, but did not open it because Frank was talking to Charley. "We been keepin' watch up north. There's shod horse tracks of three riders enterin' Cache Cañon."

Charley nodded. He'd tracked the stage robbers almost that far, but Frank had more to say.

"We tied the horses back a ways and snuck into the cañon, keepin' to the trees and shadows. They was up on that rim overlookin' the cañon with surveying tools."

Charley leaned forward. Frank still wasn't quite finished.

"Judah, me, and the riders we had along stayed hid and watched. You know anythin' about surveyin', Charley?"

"No."

"Well, years back we had a surveyor from Denver come down an' survey our west range. I went with him. He surveyed in a straight line. Them strangers atop the bluff was usin' their surveyin' tool more like it was a telescope. They kept movin' it. They were surveyin' Cache Cañon with one feller holdin' the wood stick, scrambling around like a goat every few minutes. They wasn't surveyin' beyond the cañon. They was surveyin' *inside* the cañon. Does that make sense to you?"

Charley had listened in silence and did not answer for a

41

long time, then all he said was: "For the railroad?"

Frank snorted. "They was surveyin' *inside* the cañon. You deaf, Charley? They wasn't surveyin' beyond it where track would be laid."

Charley looked steadily at Frank. "You're right, that don't make sense."

Frank nodded. "That's what I mean. The railroad wouldn't go up into that cañon. It's blocked to the north by a solid cliff of stone, an' it's too narrow for a train to go around from one side to the other to get back out."

Up to this point Judah P. had maintained his silence. Now he broke it. "I don't believe they're railroad surveyors. Can you write Denver an' find out?"

Charley gazed at the lanky Terwilliger. "That's a good idea, Judah. I'll do it."

Frank slowly turned and put a cold gaze on his brother. Charley headed off possible friction by telling Judah P. he'd never thought of that before. He even smiled as he said it and shoved out his hand. Judah P. cast a furtive look at Frank as he walked over to shake the lawman's hand. He had lost his sullen look.

After the brothers had departed, Charley searched for the railroad company's address in Denver. Then it took him almost half an hour to write the letter. Finally he walked across the street to Crittenden's Emporium and posted it.

Charley had barely returned to the jailhouse when Jim Neely showed up, clearly agitated. "If them strangers don't feed the horses I let 'em have, don't take decent care of 'em. . . ."

"They got reason to look after 'em," Charley interrupted. "They're all they got to get around on."

Neely left without further protest but not at all reassured. Charley went up to the harness shop, thinking that his job had become far too troublesome since the arrival of the strangers.

He found Jed Ames covering a half hide on his work table with the tin templates he used to cut the leather. When Charley entered, Jed ran both hands down his apron. "Nice day, Charley."

The older man ignored that. "You remember you said you'd ride out with me?"

"I did. You ready?"

"First thing in the morning, Jed, before sunrise."

"Where we goin'?"

"To Cache Cañon and roundabout up there. Frank Terwilliger was in. He, his brother, and their riders went up to that area, snuck around, hidin', and watched those surveyors, or whatever they are. Turns out they're usin' a surveyin' instrument like a telescope inside the cañon."

Jed removed his apron and got them both a cup of black java. "You should know that Jim Neely was in earlier to pick up some harness, and he told me he has half a notion to get a warrant for horse stealin' against them strangers."

Charley hadn't heard mention of anything about a warrant from Neely. He disposed of the subject by telling Jed that the liveryman had already been to the jailhouse as worried as a hen with chicks. He then dropped a clanger on the harness maker. "Jed, two of them men may be criminals. There could be warrants out on 'em already."

Jed sipped coffee. "Might not be a good idea to go up there . . . just the two of us." He sipped coffee again. "You got any idea what they're about?"

Charley didn't and emptied his cup. He went as far as the doorway. "A little before sunup, Jed," he reminded and left.

Ames refilled his cup halfway, went around the counter to his work table, and stood there. He mused that if two of those strangers were outlaws, there was a good chance that so was the third, and outlaws were usually gun handy. He shrugged, drained the cup, and leaned to place tin patterns on the tanned hide. He moved them often so that, when he cut, the amount of scrap leather would be kept to a minimum.

Something most folks did not know about Jed Ames was that he'd been gun guard for Wells Fargo and Company for six years. Charley Bent knew it, though, and he knew that Jed, too, was gun handy.

Charley was at the jailhouse, pushing a Winchester into a saddle boot when Sam Brennen came in, his face set in an unpleasant expression. He barely nodded. "I figure I got a right to ask, Charley. Why are you still in town while them bastards who robbed my coach is gettin' farther an' farther away?"

Charley made no attempt to answer until he had the saddle gun secure in its boot and had leaned it against the wall below the gun rack. Then he went to his desk, sat down, and motioned for Brennen to take a chair. Sam didn't. He was about to speak again when Charley beat him to it.

"I know where the highwaymen went . . . in what direction, anyway . . . an' I'm still in town because finding your highwaymen keeps me here."

Brennen's eyebrows shot up, his gaze fixed on the constable. "You think them bastards are citizens of Rock City?"

Charley rose without answering, only excusing himself because he had to go over to the Emporium. He left the door open on his way out.

George Crittenden was helping his clerk stack shelves. He looked around annoyedly until he saw who it was, then climbed down, straightened his vest with the massive gold watch chain, and proceeded down the counter to where Charley was standing. "What can I do for you, Constable?"

"Nothin' right now, George, but I wanted you to know that directly we're goin' to have a talk."

Crittenden watched every step Charley made as he left and walked across to the jailhouse, fished forth a large bandanna, and mopped his forehead. Then he returned to helping the clerk, but he was short with his answers. The clerk, a puny man who had worked at the store for five years, knew his employer's moods. He worked beside Crittenden in silence until they were finished, then he went out back to sweep off the loading dock. He judged it was a very good time to go out back and sweep. Crittenden was clearly worried about something.

Once Charley reëntered the jailhouse, he found Sam Brennen was gone and breathed a sigh of relief before sitting down at the desk. He waited a while, going over what he had seen and heard, until, satisfied, he went back up to the harness shop.

Jed wagged his head. "I'll be there, Charley. Quit worryin'."

"I got to raise the ante, Jed. If you still want to ride with me, come down to the jailhouse after supper."

The harness maker knew his man. "What is it, Charley?"

"It's a long story. We can talk about it when I see if George leaves town after dark. If he does, we're goin' to shag him."

Jed's eyebrows shot up. "George Crittenden?"

"Yes. He may not leave. In that case, we'll both grab some sleep. But if he does sneak out of town after dark, we'll be following. All right?"

"Sure, all right."

After the constable departed, Jed rolled and lighted a smoke, something he rarely did. *George Crittenden . . . for Christ's sake!*

At his Pleasure Palace, Cork Finney was lighting a fresh stogie when Charley walked in. They were the only two in the saloon. Cork's regulars wouldn't show up until after supper. He set a bottle and a glass in front of Charley without being asked for it. Cork blew fragrant smoke, waiting as Charley poured himself a drink. He, too, knew his man, but, when the silence ran on, Cork got impatient. "Did the Terwilligers come for their pistols?"

Charley nodded and asked a question of his own. "You know anything about George Crittenden?"

"Like what, Charley?"

"Well, anythin' underhanded and sly."

Cork removed the cigar from his mouth. "His prices, for one thing, are highway robbery."

Charley looked stonily across the bar at Cork.

Finney reddened but continued: "Local gossip . . . an' you've likely heard the same. Otherwise, I never much cared for George. He damned rarely comes to the saloon . . . Charley, what are you fishin' for?"

"Anything unusual you might know about him, anything you suspect."

Cork bit down on the stogie and thought a moment. "If anybody'd know, it'd be Sam Brennen. He goes a hunnert miles to buy horseshoes for less money than George charges. He don't like George any more than I do."

Charley went out front, gazing over at the corral yard. He really did not want to ask Sam the question he'd just put to Cork Finney for an elementary reason — Cork inhaled a lot of talk and exhaled little of it. Most of the time Sam was like a tight-wound spring, and he had a tongue hinged in the middle that flapped at both ends. If he thought Charley had an idea Crittenden was involved in something illegal, he'd spread it all over town. Charley decided, instead, to return to the jailhouse.

Rock City remained quiet, and Charley had no interruptions for the balance of the day. Enjoying his solitude, he considered the booted Winchester, pocketed a couple of tins of canned sardines, and for some reason he was never able to explain, even to himself, he filled a canteen and hung it from a wall peg near the saddle gun. There were creeks and trickling veins of water where he thought they might ride.

He had an early supper that he brought over to the office from the café, pulled a chair to the small, barred, front window, sat down, and watched people come and go over at the Emporium. He also reviewed the logic that was behind what he intended to do. He considered two events, neither of which was critical. One was that he'd seen the three strangers enter the store. They'd spent about an hour in there before they emerged. When asked, Crittenden had said all they'd bought was tobacco. Yet, George had acted oddly when Charley had mentioned the three. The other suspicion he had was even less tangible. Crittenden had been noticeably avoiding Charley. Heretofore, he would walk over frequently, sometimes to bring mail, other times to sit and gossip.

If any other lawmen were to hear Charley's reasons, he would have laughed at him until he was red in the face. Maybe Charley was reaching for straws. On the other hand, the strangers had not openly returned to town for several days, although they had clandestinely moved their belongings from the hotel. Jim Neely's horses would make out all right in the open, but their riders couldn't eat grass. Somebody would have to take out grub to them.

Jed came by on his way back from the livery barn. He reported that Neely was still stirred up about his horses. Jed wanted to confirm that their early morning ride was still on. Charley nodded and told him that he had been thinking about just that. He suggested they should meet down at the livery barn before dawn, unless Crittenden left town before that. If he'd told the harness maker his reasons for believing they might have to follow Crittenden, Jed would not have said it, but he would have regarded their proposed jaunt as senseless.

Once Jed left, Charley's own misgivings increased. He went

to the saloon to settle his nerves. Since he appeared so preoccupied, the saloonman left him alone. Charley saw the Terwilliger brothers at the bar. Frank nodded, but Judah P. studied his own reflection in the back-bar mirror as though unaware of the constable's presence. All this time Cork was sweating. He hadn't been informed by either party that the Terwilligers had pretty much ironed out their differences with Charley when the constable had returned their guns. When some range men came in, Cork set out a bottle and a row of little glasses. Otherwise, he kept watching Charley and the Terwilligers. But Charley, while he had acknowledged Frank's nod and had nodded in return, was too lost in thought to be diverted even by Frank and Judah P.

Only when Charley left after a single night cap did Cork relax. He and the Terwilligers exchanged words, and Cork could not hide his astonishment when Judah P. remarked: "Charley Bent's a good lawman." After all, Judah P. still had a swollen, though fading, discoloration from when Charley had downed him.

Charley did not go up to his room at the hotel. Instead, from the jailhouse he continued to watch for sign that George Crittenden was leaving town. None came and, eventually, he slept fitfully at the desk. What brought him wide awake was the chill. A glance at the wall clock told him it was about time to go down to the livery barn and meet Jed.

Rock City was nearly lightless and couldn't have been more quiet than if it had been one of those ghost towns scattered throughout the territories. Jed was waiting. His horse stood hip-shot, asleep. When Charley appeared, Jed did not say how long he'd waited, but he led his horse out back and mounted him.

Charley rigged out without awakening the liveryman's hired nighthawk. In the chill air he and Jed went north until they left Rock City, then they veered off the roadway and made their way overland in darkness.

Jed said: "You figure to explain this, Charley?"

The constable's reply sounded almost defensive. "Them strangers visited with George Crittenden. He told me they'd only come in for tobacco. Jed, they was in there with George close to an hour."

Jed considered this without comment. He leaned to free a buckle of his booted saddle gun that had caught on a fender.

Charley explained everything, and, while Jed listened, his expression was hidden by the darkness. Eventually he said: "Did you see Crittenden leave town?"

"Well no, but. . . ."

"He didn't leave town, Charley, but he did somethin' Jim Neely thought was almighty unusual. You know he keeps his drivin' horse an' buggy at the livery barn. Yesterday afternoon he got the outfit rigged out an' drove up the back alley behind the store. I went over there before I went down to wait for you. The buggy's parked next to the loadin' dock, and the horse is in a shed across the alley."

Charley digested this information without speaking, then he reined to a halt. "Why'n hell didn't you tell me before we left town?"

"Because I figure a man who says he'll meet me at the barn before daylight, an' says as how we might have to shag after Crittenden, must know somethin' I don't. You want to go back?"

Without answering, Charley reined around and started toward town. He was irritated that Jed hadn't told him about Crittenden sooner. Yet, it was his own fault. *He* had fallen asleep, and hadn't known beforehand whether Crittenden had left town or not.

Chapter Five

THE BUGGY WITH YELLOW WHEELS

They kept the vigil for two more nights. The morning of the third day Charley went into the eastside alley and strode northward, hoping he wouldn't be noticed. The top buggy with yellow wheels and red running gear was still where they had seen it parked. Charley went up to the harness shop where Jed offered coffee as he said: "You get the feelin' we're chasin' a pipe dream?"

Charley might have agreed, except that the buggy hadn't been returned to the livery barn. He mentioned this and added: "Why would he park it next to the loadin' dock?"

Jed conceded but without grace. "Thing is, Charley, if he don't leave town for a week, you 'n' me are both goin' to sleep through it."

Charley returned to the jailhouse. He was just finishing up some long-neglected paperwork when Jim Neely appeared. "I want a warrant out for them strangers for horse stealin'," Neely said anxiously. "It's been a week, Charley."

The constable got into his desk chair and leaned back. "In the first place," he said, "you don't know they stole your horses. In the second place, I'd have to find 'em to serve a warrant."

"Sam Brennen told me you figure someone in town is workin' with them three."

"I didn't tell him any such damned thing," Charley replied irritably.

Neely hadn't expected anger. He went as far as the door before asking if Charley meant to find his horses. Charley's

50

reply was tentative. "Maybe in a day or two."

Neely left the constable's office in a sullen mood. Shortly after his departure, Charley went over to the café for his midday meal. Except for the slovenly proprietor, the place was empty. Charley ordered, and, when the platter of food and coffee arrived, he leaned over the counter. Behind him the main street door opened and closed. He did not look around. He was hungry. Also he was not in a good mood. It did not improve when Jed Ames sat beside him at the counter and said: "The buggy's gone."

Charley chased down a swallow of meat with the coffee and looked at the man beside him.

Jed asked then: "Where'd you get the notion he'd leave in the night?"

Charley ignored the question to ask one of his own. "How long ago?"

"I don't know. I'd guess a few hours back. I just happened to be takin' a breedin' harness to the feller who's got a stallion on the road behind the store. I looked over toward the rear of the Emporium, an' the buggy an' its horse was gone."

Charley started to get up.

"If you figure to ask George's clerk, I already have. He told me George wasn't there when he came to work."

Charley, who had eaten less than half his meal, stepped back, dropped some coins beside the platter, and jerked his head. The two men left the café together. Outside, Charley told Jed that, since it was full daylight and the country he figured Crittenden would cross was flat for miles, it should be not only possible to find Crittenden but even to overtake him.

Without a word Jed crossed the street and walked southward in the direction of the livery barn. Charley followed him. Upon their arrival, they were told by the day hosteler that Neely had left a couple of hours ago to find those strangers and his horses.

51

The day hosteler watched the constable and his companion rig out their horses. The constable owned his mount, but the harness maker didn't. The day hosteler wanted to mention this to Jed, but neither of the two men saddling up looked like they'd be interested. In fact, to the day hosteler, they looked downright unfriendly.

Charley and Jed rode out of town as they'd done previously, up the westside alley to the stage road. The sun was high and only slightly off center. They left the road where a single set of buggy tracks crossed the berm. No other such tracks had shown up before.

Charley was anxious. If he was right and Crittenden was supplying the three strangers, he wanted to overtake the top buggy before it rendezvoused with the strangers, two of whom were now suspected outlaws.

As they loped, Charley unburdened himself, and Jed listened. Afterwards Jed asked: "Why didn't you hang their hides out to dry when they was in town?"

"Because I got to have extradition papers for the Smith feller, and they got to convince the governor of Colorado they got good reason, and Brownsville's down in Texas, so I wait." He also told Jed about the scrap of paper from the hotel that Mart Kemp had brought to him. "There's no date, an' if there was a heading, it had been torn off."

Jed rode in thought half a mile before bursting out scornfully: "The law! Things was better years back."

Charley neither agreed nor disagreed. He had caught sight of a moving speck in the distance. They increased their gait but had to rein back several times to blow the horses.

They were now crossing open grassland. That worried Jed more than it did the constable. Charley's concern was to overtake the top buggy. They got close enough to identify the rig, and Jed began watching the foothills up near Cache Cañon.

He had his six-gun but not his carbine. The last time they slackened off they were almost within rifle range. There was no mistaking the Crittenden buggy.

Then Jed abruptly raised an arm. "Look!"

Three horsemen were standing with their animals at the mouth of Cache Cañon. Charley had a diversionary thought — at least he had found Jim Neely's horses. That thought was instantly followed by another. Neither he nor Jed had their saddle guns. He hoped the three strangers didn't, either, but that was something Charley wouldn't want to bet his life on.

The buggy stopped. Crittenden got out, facing in the direction of the constable and his companion. He had halted about three-quarters of a mile from the waiting men at Cache Cañon. Charley and Jed closed the intervening distance at a lope. George Crittenden seemed to have taken root. He had recognized his pursuers.

Jed wasn't worried about Crittenden. He'd never seen him wearing a sidearm. But those distant strangers were another matter. When they reached the buggy and rode up along the left side, Charley noticed the small space for luggage behind the seat was covered with a tied-down canvas.

Crittenden had never been a good actor. He tipped down his hat to avoid sun glare. "Well, now, I never seen you boys this far from town before." What was supposed to be an ebullient statement sounded palpably false, but the paunchy storekeeper still tried to carry off his bluff demeanor. "Beautiful day. Clear as glass."

The constable looked steadily at the storekeeper as he said: "Take the canvas off, George."

Crittenden procrastinated. "It's nothin' but some store goods, Charley."

"Take the canvas off!"

Crittenden was sweating, possibly not altogether from the

hot sunlight, as he went to remove the canvas. While he was loosening the anchoring ropes, he shot a surreptitious glance in the direction of the men at the mouth of Cache Cañon.

Jed said dryly: "You lookin' for someone, George?"

Crittenden neither answered nor looked northward again. When he peeled back the canvas, Charley and the harness maker gazed at the supplies, which included tinned peaches, sourdough bread in one of those large round loaves that were popular, two cartons of bullets, one each for hand guns and for saddle guns. There were also additional foodstuffs wrapped in some blankets. Enough to last three men a long time.

Jed was staring northward when Charley slowly dismounted for a closer look at the supplies. He said quietly: "What did you figure to do, George, set up a camp for yourself?"

Crittenden's usually pale face was pink. He would not look at the constable when he spoke. "I'm not much given to campin'."

Charley went to remount his horse. "Remember me tellin' you one of these days we'd have to talk?"

Crittenden bobbed his head like an apple on a string.

Charley next spoke from the saddle. "Jed an' I'll outride for you on the way back to town."

As Crittenden was preparing to climb into the buggy, Jed observed: "Here they come, Charley."

Crittenden didn't climb in. He stood with his back to Charley and Jed and watched the oncoming riders. He might have made a statement, but his mind was frozen.

Charley surprised Jed by saying: "Let's go meet them."

Jed stared, but when Charley urged his horse ahead, he followed and silently cursed the constable for not bringing along more riders from town.

With both parties riding at a lope, the distance between them closed rapidly. They met about a quarter mile from

Crittenden and his buggy. The last time Charley had seen the strangers only one had been bearded. Now the other two showed a healthy stubble. They obviously hadn't shaved in days.

Jed watched the one called Smith. He was the first to speak when they met. He was a better actor than George Crittenden. He smiled and nodded before speaking. "You 'n' the storekeeper in some kind of tangle?"

Charley did not take his eyes off the other men. "Not a tangle exactly. The liveryman in town wants a warrant out for you gents."

"What for?" Smith asked, showing surprise.

"You owe him for them rented horses an' haven't either returned 'em or paid him."

For the first time Al Shokely intervened. He laughed. "He didn't tell us there was a time limit on returnin' the horses, Constable. When we're through, we'll bring 'em back. Look at 'em. They're in as good a shape as when he let us have 'em."

That part was true enough. Among the supplies in Crittenden's buggy was a sack of rolled barley.

Smith said: "Tell you what," and groped in a trouser pocket from which he brought forth a pad of greenbacks. He counted out several of them and held them out. "This is about what we owe him. Tell him we'll be along directly to settle up." Smith smiled. "Do we look like horse thieves, Constable? Because we ain't."

Charley took the bank notes and tucked them into a shirt pocket. The horse theft item had been resolved. He asked Smith if he and his friends were camped up yonder and got what he considered to be a prepared answer. "We move around a lot an' make camp in a lot of different places."

Charley asked: "Cache Cañon?"

Smith's geniality died. "Mostly elsewhere. You got a reason for askin' questions, Constable?"

Charley shook his head slowly and asked another question. "Are them supplies Crittenden's loaded up with for you gents?"

Smith nodded. "Yep. Don't worry. We'll pay the storekeeper when we get 'em."

Charley was reining around as he said: "I hope you got a way to get them wherever your camp is, because the storekeeper's goin' to unload 'em where he stands. He's going back with us."

If Charley had looked around as he rode in the direction of the top buggy, he would have seen three men watching him depart with expressionless faces. They remained at that quarter-mile distance while Charley and Jed helped Crittenden unload. Crittenden didn't object. In fact, he seemed relieved. The only time he acknowledged the riders in the near distance was just before climbing into the buggy. He raised his right arm toward them. They did not return the salute.

On the way back to town Crittenden wanted to talk, an additional indication of his relief. But, getting no response from his outriders, he eventually gave it up.

It was one of those days that had started out hot and got steadily hotter — not exactly unheard of, with autumn approaching, but not commonplace, either. By the time they saw Rock City, the stud-necked, big, seal-brown mare, pulling the buggy, was sweating even around the eyes.

While Charley pushed Crittenden toward the jailhouse, Jed offered to take care of the horses, which he did by tying the saddle animals to the tailgate and leading the docile large mare. When Jim Neely saw Jed coming, he became confused by the absence of George Crittenden in the buggy. But his main concern was the other animals, and, as Jed handed him the reins to the constable's horse and the one he had ridden, Neely could not contain himself any longer.

"Did you find them rascals, Jed?"

Jed was stripping the California harness off the big mare as he answered. "We found 'em. One of 'em gave Charley money for you." When Neely turned toward the wide, front doorway, Jed called to him: "I wouldn't go up there just yet. Wait an hour or so."

It was good advice. Charley was both rough and brusque with George Crittenden. First, he shoved him down in a chair, then he went to the desk and sat down on top of it, looking coldly toward the merchant. He didn't speak. He didn't have to. Crittenden said: "Far as I know, it's no crime to deliver goods to folks."

Charley leaned back. "George, let me tell you somethin'. In this world there's two kinds of people I got no use for. One is liars. The other is thieves." He leaned back on the desk. "Tell me about your connection with those surveyors."

"Connection? What connection?"

Charley stood up. He was a large, imposing man. "When they come to town, they spent an hour at your store. You told me all they bought was tobacco, and, while we was talkin', you acted nervous about something."

"That's all they did buy . . . a couple of sacks of Bull Durham."

"It took you an hour to sell a couple of sacks of Bull Durham?"

Crittenden fidgeted with the gold chain across his middle. "All right, they gave me a list of supplies they'd need, an' I said I'd deliver 'em. Is that against the law?"

"They was at your store, George, almost two weeks ago, an' just today you took 'em supplies?"

Charley remained standing. They looked at each other until Charley started toward Crittenden, then the storekeeper said:

"They had a map . . . asked me if I could read it. I did. It was a pretty ragged piece of paper, but the lines made sense. I told them it looked to me to be directions to Cache Cañon. The bearded feller . . . his name's Bill Smith . . . gave me a silver dollar, an' they left."

"And you was to deliver their supplies to Cache Cañon?"

"Yes, but not until a few days later did they tell me where to deliver 'em."

So far, Charley had little reason to disbelieve Crittenden, but his next question made the paunchy storekeeper squirm. "They came to the store several times, didn't they?"

"Yes."

"George, don't lie to me. Did you an' them strangers make some kind of deal?"

Crittenden stopped twisting the watch chain and regarded the constable from a sweaty face. He hung fire before answering. "You've heard how the valley an' that draw in the foothills got their name?"

Charley had heard that tale not once but many times, and he put about as much faith in it as did most other folks. He said: "Someone . . . old-time Spaniards . . . a band of outlaws . . . even the Indians . . . supposedly hid a big cache of gold an' what not. Is that what they're lookin' for?"

Crittenden nodded, and Charley sat down in the chair behind his desk. Folks had been digging holes in so many places over the years until the most fervent treasure-hunter among them gave up searching and called the old story some early day explorer's idea of either an outright lie or a joke.

He pushed himself forward, looking steadily at the storekeeper. Before he could speak, Crittenden turned defensive. "The map led straight to Cache Cañon. I got no idea where they got it, but I can tell you this . . . they believed it was a true map to the cache." Crittenden paused to wipe his face with a large, blue bandanna. "Last time we talked, they promised to give me a share if I'd supply 'em."

Charley wagged his head. "I thought you was too good a businessman to . . . ? Did you agree, supplies for a share?"

"Yes, Charley. They believe they know where the cache is. I figured I couldn't lose much, if I gave 'em supplies, and, if they found a cache, I'd most likely be rich."

"Do you know anythin' about those men, George? I mean, who they are . . . what they've done?"

"Well, I was raised to know that it's not polite to ask personal questions."

Charley leaned far back, almost imperceptibly shaking his head.

Crittenden reddened. He remained defensive. "I've been a storekeeper for close to thirty years. I been tired of it for almost as long. How many times in a man's life does something like this happen to him? Charley, it's damned well worth the gamble."

"Do you believe, if they find a cache, they're goin' to look you up an' give you a share?" When Crittenden didn't answer, Charley added: "After what happened up there today, they're goin' to want to ask you some questions. If you tell 'em about our talk . . . if they don't kill you . . . I'll make up charges that'll send you to prison for the rest of your life."

Crittenden rose. "You got my word. I won't say a thing, but there's got to be some reason I can give them as to why you stopped me out yonder."

"Tell a lie, George. I doubt if it'll be your first. Tell 'em, I thought you was runnin' guns to them hold-outs that're supposed to be up there. You could even warn them about the Indians."

Crittenden nodded vigorously. He liked Charley's suggestion.

"A word of warning, George. You better make sure they believe you, because I can tell you this much . . . if they don't believe you, they'll kill you."

Crittenden nodded while sidling toward the door.

Charley made one more comment. "You're playin' with fire. Make the lie believable."

After the storekeeper left, Charley rose, went to the small, barred window, and gazed in the direction of the Emporium. If he'd told Crittenden what he knew about the strangers, he would be so nervous when they met again, they would suspect something and likely shoot him. From what Charley suspected about those strangers, they wouldn't hesitate.

Chapter Six

THE ARRIVAL OF DAYLIGHT

Jim Neely arrived at the jailhouse before dusk, slightly breathless and looking hopeful. Charley fished the greenbacks from his shirt pocket and tossed them across the desk where Neely grabbed at them like the devil after a crippled saint. He was full of gratitude.

Charley was hungry. He eased Neely out after telling him his horses looked good and were being grained. Also he reminded him: "Every day they don't return your animals is as good as money in your pocket."

Then Charley left to catch a bite to eat. At the café Jed Ames was already having supper. He looked up when Charley entered, nodded, and went back to his meal. As Charley eased down, he mentioned giving the greenbacks to Jim Neely. Jed continued eating. He wasn't interested in the liveryman.

After the constable's platter and coffee arrived, Jed said: "An' George?"

Charley was gazing at his meal as he answered. "It's a long story, Jed. If you want to come over to the jailhouse later, I'll explain it to you."

"You didn't lock him up?" Jed asked.

Charley looked pained. "For what? It's not against the law to haul supplies."

"He didn't tell you any more?"

Charley finally attacked his platter. "Later, over at the jailhouse."

That meeting never happened. Jed left the café and some-

61

time later so did the constable. They both had the same destination — Cork Finney's Pleasure Palace. When they met up there, Charley took a bottle and two jolt glasses to a distant table where both he and Jed Ames sat down.

Jed waited. Charley filled both their glasses before beginning his tale. Neither man touched the whiskey until Charley was finished with what he had to say. Then Jed downed his, blew out a flammable breath, and spoke for the first time since they'd sat at the table.

"George can't be that dumb," he said. "He's been dealin' with people a long time. He sure as hell must have had misgivings about them three."

Charley had thought the same thing. In fact, he had said as much to the storekeeper, and now he told Jed: "To you an' me it might sound too good, but not to George. He's gettin' long in the tooth. He's sick an' tired of runnin' the store. Like he told me, what they offered him was hope and his last chance to make a lot of money."

Jed was not swayed. "But them strangers wouldn't have to give him a share. If they found a cache, there'd be a good reason for them to just up an' leave the country." Then Jed asked Charley what he was going to do.

Charley's answer was simple. "Nothin', until I got reason. They got as much right as you have to hunt the cache."

That didn't satisfy Jed, either, but he refilled the little glasses before replying. "There's got to be a way. You figure that one's a bank robber an' another one most likely killed a man, his wife, and his little girl."

Charley did not down the second jolt. He looked around the room and back. Before he could speak, Frank Terwilliger burst into the saloon, saw the constable, and came to the table.

"I got a dead rider in front of the jailhouse," Frank told the constable. "Judah P.'s with him."

Charley arose to follow Terwilliger out. Jed emptied his little glass before following the constable.

It was growing dark. Charley had to fetch a lamp from the jailhouse. Neither of the Terwilligers spoke. They didn't have to. There was a small, bloody, puckered spot about three inches above the cowboy's eyes. He had probably been dead before he hit the ground. Charley looked across the wagon bed.

Judah P. said: "He's the feller we had at the north line shack. His name was Watson. Constable, you want me to guess? He run onto them surveyors before. Life at a line shack gets damned tiresome. My guess is that he snuck around to see what them strangers was doin', an' one of them shot him."

Frank spoke next. "No proof, Constable, but he sure as hell didn't shoot himself, an' as far as I know them three is the only other ones up there."

Jed shook his head and departed. Lately he'd been missing too much sleep.

Charley emptied the dead man's pockets, found nothing a range man wouldn't be carrying, and told the Terwilligers to take the body to the carpenter's shop. The carpenter was also the local undertaker. Dr. Reese, the town doctor and coroner, must also be sent for.

Frank jerked his head for Judah P. to do as the constable had suggested, while he followed Charley into the jailhouse where he dropped a worn, old six-shooter on the desk. "Ain't been fired," he said.

"Watson's gun?"

Frank nodded, sought a chair, and sat down. It required more to get Frank Terwilliger fired up than it did most men, but now, seeing his face half shadowed by the hanging lamp, Charley wasn't surprised to find a coldness in Frank's eyes even though he did not raise his voice.

63

"If you won't do it, Constable, my brother 'n' me an' our riders will."

"Do what?"

"Find them three, pistol whip 'em until they admit who shot Watson, an' then hang the son-of-a-bitch."

Charley sighed. This was not going to be easy, but he had to do it. He began quietly. "Frank, it's my job, not yours."

"Does that mean you're goin' after 'em?"

"I can go talk to 'em, but unless there's proof they shot Watson, there's damned little I can do."

Frank got angry. "For Christ's sake, who else could have done it?"

"That's not proof."

Frank rose from the chair and turned to leave. "You do what you got to do, an' so will we," he promised. He was at the door when Charley stopped him.

"Frank, there's somethin' you ought to know. It seems likely that two of those strangers are wanted men, an' I've yet to see a range man or a townsman who could survive a shoot-out with their kind."

Frank didn't move. "You know two of them bastards are wanted men, and you sit on your butt, doin' nothin'?"

"I'm goin' after them," Charley replied, "but, until I get proof, there's not a hell of a lot I *can* do."

"Then why go after 'em? Constable, you just go on settin' here. Don't show up on the north range."

After Frank had slammed the door upon departing, Charley swore a blue streak. How long was it going to be before he got notice that the governor of Colorado had signed extradition papers on Smith? He went to his room at the hotel to sleep, but only ended up pounding the pillow. After several restless hours, Charley gave it up.

Back at the jailhouse, while it was still darker outside than the inside of a boot, he lighted the hanging lantern. Its light was feeble and spotty. No one had cleaned and trimmed the wick in a coon's age.

Without a warning someone fired a gun. It had been close, near the jailhouse. Actually it didn't necessarily have to bode ill. People shot at night at marauding varmints of many kinds. Charley went outside. It was impossible to place exactly where that one shot had been fired. The buildings showed no light, but several town dogs were raising hell and even propping it up. Charley went back for a sawed-off shotgun and then proceeded up one side of the town street and then down the other side. He found nothing and heard nothing.

A light came on over at the café. When he knocked at the door until the caféman opened it, he made a lasting impression. Charley was not only big enough to eat hay, but he was standing wide-legged in the doorway, holding a scatter-gun.

The caféman habitually rose early to fire up the cook stove. He didn't find his tongue until the constable asked if he'd heard a gunshot, then the caféman nodded vigorously. He'd heard it.

"Which direction did it come from?"

The caféman had no idea but offered to rassle up breakfast for the lawman. Charley left him peering out the open door.

When daylight came and Rock City slowly resumed its normal routines, it turned out just about everyone had heard the gunshot. Generally it was attributed to some householder shooting a varmint for rooting in a garbage can, which was not altogether unusual. Little more was made of the incident. Not until George Crittenden's skinny clerk came to the jailhouse, white to the hairline. The sense of shock was so profound the clerk didn't raise his voice when he said: "Mister Crittenden is dead. He's been shot, Constable."

Charley and the clerk crossed to the Emporium. Crittenden

had been in his small, cluttered office. He had a cot there, but seldom used it. He generally slept in the house he owned. As the badly shaken clerk watched, Charley raised the dead man's head by the hair. The bullet had been fired at sufficiently close range for there to be powder burns on Crittenden's shirt. The slug had hit the storekeeper dead center. Like the Terwilligers' range man, Crittenden had been killed instantly.

As it always did with something like this, the news spread rapidly. In fact, while Charley was concluding his examination, several people, all male, crowded into the store. Charley brusquely chased them out. He told the clerk to lock the front door and keep it locked and to get Dr. Reese to examine the body. Charley then went back over to the jailhouse, got the booted Winchester, and, carrying it over his shoulder, went up to the harness shop. Jed was rolling leather cut-outs into moist rags. He stopped what he was doing and stared.

Charley said: "Let's ride. This time I think we better take some others."

Jed hadn't heard about the killing. While it shocked him, in view of what Charley had told him the previous evening, he wasn't totally surprised. He wiped his hands, nodded, and went into his lean-to living quarters out back for his gun belt. This time he also took his Winchester.

There had been talk among the townsmen of the Terwilliger line rider having been killed, but the shooting of a man most of them had known for many years, whether they liked him or not, was an outrage. None had ever seen George Crittenden carry a sidearm, and that included Jed Ames and Constable Bent. Although no one liked murder and many were loud in their denunciation of the crime, when the constable sought posse riders, he was only able to recruit a few willing men. The majority of townsmen he talked to either had a sick wife or child, or were coming down with something themselves.

A few folks were wrapped against the brisk morning air as they stood like wooden Indians on both sides of the street, watching the posse leave town. Of those willing to help, no one asked where Charley was leading them. They assumed — correctly — he knew, and that was good enough. Andy Buck was along, pleased that at last Charley was going to do something about the bank robber he'd identified.

Jed was riding beside the local butcher when he said: "It's finally comin' to a head."

The butcher looked at Jed. "What's comin' to a head?"

Saying no more, Jed kneed his livery mount up beside the constable's. They rode together in silence.

There were seven in the posse, and most, like the butcher, were not seasoned posse riders. Jed mentioned this, and Charley replied: "They just might have to learn awful fast."

"You think it was the strangers who done it?"

"You know someone killed a Terwilliger rider yesterday. He was at their north line shack, and was shot between the eyes. Maybe them strangers didn't do it, but like Frank said, who else? No one else has been seen there."

"So you figure George might have been killed by his partners, searchin' for the cache?"

"As good a guess as any. I'd like for once an' all to get this business of them strangers straightened out."

Cork Finney was along. He had locked the saloon, which would not be appreciated by his regulars, but, while Cork hadn't liked George Crittenden, as was true of the others he liked murder less.

After a time Charley left the roadway in the direction of the foothills. When he did this, it finally became obvious to the posse men where he was leading them. Not all his riders knew much about the strangers, and until Charley had Cache Cañon in sight he did not tell them about the Terwilliger rider and his suspicions. No one asked questions, although they had believed they were seeking the storekeeper's killer. There was a little subdued conversation. If they hadn't thought they were only seeking Crittenden's killer, perhaps at least half of them would not have joined the posse.

Now the sun was up over the eastern horizon like a seed popped out of a grape. Jed was studying the foothills. It bothered him that an obviously well-armed posse would be seen, provided the strangers were watching.

Andy Buck stood in his stirrups. "Hell, I know that place. Me 'n' some other damned fools went up there lookin' for that cache. All we found was rocks an' rattlesnakes." The blacksmith eased down in his saddle. "There's an old, log shack an' a tumble-down pole corral up there, though."

The butcher laughed. "What'd you do with the gold, Andy?"

The blacksmith did not reply. In fact, for a half mile no one spoke until, close to the mouth of the cañon, someone asked if this was where the Terwilliger rider had been shot. Charley had to say he didn't know. By this time he and others, not just Jed, were studying the tilted country ahead with its draws and gullies.

A nervous Ray Kemp said: "Charley? This is good bushwhackin' country."

Charley didn't comment, but that suggestion made them all ride a little straighter in the saddle.

The sun was above them as they approached the mouth of Cache Cañon.

Cork Finney said abruptly: "There's birds singin', Charley."

The constable nodded. For a fact, they could hear birds up the cañon. Where there were men, there usually weren't birds close by.

Charley led them at a dead walk past the mouth of the cañon. The birds flew off. Then there was total silence.

Jed offered to scout ahead. Charley told the harness maker to stay where he was and led the way himself. The posse riders behind him did not speak. They were peering intently up the stony slopes, and one or two yanked their six-gun tie-downs loose.

They saw the tumble-down, old house and its even more dilapidated lodgepole pine corral. Charley halted abruptly. He thought he had seen a brief movement on the far side of the house. He fisted his six-gun, held it in his lap, and then rode ahead. The others followed.

Coming nearer, it was apparent that the place was deserted. The strangers were nowhere about and neither were their horses.

The posse scattered to explore both sides of the cañon and up as far as the formidable, high-frowning bluff at the northern end. Here, Cork Finney made a discovery and called attention to it. When Charley came up, Cork pointed to a very old trail hugging around the side hill, heading for the bluff. There was recent sign of hoof marks of boots in its ancient dust.

Charley looked up the trail. Once there might have been three surveyors up there. Now there was only an eagle, soaring high.

They returned to the log house, dismounted, and stood beside their horses to palaver. It seemed obvious — the three strangers had gone up that trail for some reason. Why they would go up there was anyone's guess, but the trail was wide enough for horsebackers.

Jed led the search through their outfits inside the old house, some blankets, dumped haphazardly, and a large supply of groceries. Jed recognized several of the grocery items. Knowing where the strangers had their Cache Cañon camp only increased Charley's wondering why they had ridden up that trail to the country above. Inevitably, someone made the comment about the strangers not knowing there were hold-out Indians up there, and so had taken a risk the posse men would not take.

Cork Finney, a sedentary individual usually, discovered how sedentary he was when he volunteered to go part way up the trail to sit and watch for the strangers. He went up it a couple of hundred yards before collapsing on a large stone. The others could see him up there. One of them called. "Farther up, Cork."

The saloonman called back a tart remark. "This trail's steeper than it looks. Fellers, our country is the only place I ever been that, no matter which way you go, it's uphill."

They watched Cork hike farther upward until they lost sight of him because of tall underbrush.

Jed was the first to help himself to the groceries. The others followed his example. There was a piddling, little creek east of the old, log house.

Charley sat in shade, eating with the others. He was particularly silent with his gaze fixed atop the cliff face. Jed read his mind.

"Why'n hell would anyone go up there at all?"

Charley had no answer. Something else worried him. The posse's horses were visible from atop the bluff. So were they.

The town butcher, unaccustomed to horsebacking, leaned against the logs, tipped down his hat, and snoozed.

One of the posse men asked if they were going to wait there until the strangers came back, and, when Charley nodded, the man had another question. "You really figure one of those fellers shot George Crittenden?"

Charley looked at him. "One of 'em likely killed that Terwilliger rider, an', while I ain't sure, I think they had reason to kill George, too."

That settled the question of why they were in Cache Cañon,

and, as long as there was graze and water for their animals and enough groceries to keep pleats from forming in their stomachs, they'd sit and wait. No one suggested riding up that trail into the wild, gloomy, and primitive uplands.

Chapter Seven

THREE DEAD MEN

Andy Buck went exploring and found several small mounds of rocks. He called to Charley who went up along a side hill where the blacksmith was waiting. Charley leaned forward to examine the mounds and then came upright again. "Somethin' them surveyors did?"

The blacksmith pointed to other rock cairns. "This close together?"

Charley, who knew little of surveying, shook his head. "Damned if I know, Andy."

Buck got down on both knees and began dismantling the mounded stones. When he was down to soil, he began digging, using one of the sharp-edged rocks from the cairn. Charley watched. Finally Buck said: "Nothin' buried here. The ground's as hard as one of these rocks."

They went back toward the cabin, and Jed, who had been watching, asked what they'd found. Charley told him. Jed's curiosity died. He went over to look at the horses. There was nothing unusual about horses unacquainted with each other to squeal and put their ears back, but no one got kicked by a hobbled horse because, when hobbled in front, a horse could not very well kick with his hind legs.

Time passed. Men and horses dozed with the sun directly overhead. It got hot in the cañon, hotter than it would be in open country. What brought them all wide awake was the echo of gunshots. First, a single shot, then several more. Cork Finney's head appeared above the underbrush. He was squinting up the trail. When he was satisfied with what he heard, he started down the trail as he yelled: "Someone's comin' fast."

Charley called back. "Stay up there, Cork. Let 'em pass you. Keep out of sight."

Cork sought cover. He had to retrace his steps before he found any. The watching men in the cañon could no longer see him. There was one more gunshot. It hadn't been as distant as the earlier gunshots.

Jed said: "They're comin', Charley."

He was right, but, when they burst into view, running and occasionally looking back, there were only two of the strangers, not three, and they were afoot.

They paused atop the cliff. The posse and horses in the cañon were the cause. Where they had expected to find sanctuary below, they saw instead a sizable party of horsemen. One of the strangers called to the other, and both again plunged down the trail. They passed Cork's hiding place clearly concerned with only one thing — getting down from the heights.

Charley told Jed to gather several of the men and disarm the strangers when they reached the floor of the cañon. In the meantime, he stood in the shade, watching the overhead bluff. Eventually what he saw did not completely surprise him. He had heard of elusive hide-out Indians with skepticism for years, but the three men who appeared now atop the cliff were not only Indians, they were armed and clearly hostile.

The butcher and the blacksmith also saw them. The butcher said softly: "I'll be damned."

Jed and some others positioned themselves where the trail met the cañon floor. When the breathless strangers came up and stopped, Jed said: "Empty your holsters, an' be damned careful how you do it."

The pair of sweat-soaked, hard-breathing strangers shucked

their guns as Al Shokely said: "There's a whole god-damned mess of Indians up there. They come at us right after we had a shoot-out with two trigger-happy ranchers. Ben plugged one of the ranchers. The other one got Ben. I plugged him. Then we was hit by a whole damned mess of Indians."

Charley walked over. They recognized him. The man called Bill Smith advised: "We better fort up, Constable."

Charley looked toward the overhead bluff. The Indians were no longer visible. He returned his attention to the strangers. "What were you doing up there?"

"We just went up to see what the country was like," Al Shokely explained. "A couple of ranchers saw us an' started shootin'. Like I said, Ben Leathergood plugged one of 'em an' got plugged himself. I shot the other one. It was a clear case of self-defense, Constable. They started the shootin' first. Then a broncho buck come out of nowhere, carryin' an old musket. I fired a shot at him, then more Indians began appearing from the trees like ghosts." Shokely paused to suck air. When he would continue, his companion interrupted.

"We done nothin'. Just explorin' a little. Them tomahawks come out of nowhere."

"You done nothin' but shoot two ranchers an' fired at an Injun," Charley replied. He jerked his head, and the strangers did not resist being taken to the old, log house.

It was crowded when everyone got inside. The expression on the faces of several posse men showed something more than anxiety. They showed fear. Shokely and Smith sat on their saddles. They passed a canteen back and forth. Their breathing was almost back to normal.

"They're up there, Charley," Cork Finney said when he entered. "I got no idea how many, but, if they shoot from the bluff, we're not in a real good position."

Another posse rider added: "If they shoot the horses an' set us afoot, for them it'll be like pickin' off pigeons on a roost."

Burly, small-eyed Al Shokely put in: "They'll come. You can bet new money on that."

Charley listened and eventually spoke. "I had a few scrapes with Injuns years back, but I'll be damned if I'm goin' to fight 'em this time. I'll hand you two over to 'em."

There was a long silence before several posse men nodded approval. Bill Smith stood up. His beard was layered with dust. "What the hell are you sayin', Constable? They're Indians! Killin' those two ranch men was self-defense. They started it."

"What about your horses?" Charley asked.

"We left 'em up there," Shokely replied. "We was afoot when those ranchers jumped us. Then the Indians started comin' at us before we could get back to the horses. We lit out for here afoot, figgering to fort up."

Charley Bent went outside where Jed and Andy Buck joined him. There was no longer anyone on the overhead bluff. Charley shook his head. "Those three been nothin' but trouble since they come here. I'll tell you for a fact the two that're left are both wanted men. If it comes to that, I meant what I said in there. The Injuns can have 'em."

Buck looked steadily at Charley. "You got any idea what they'll do to 'em? I wouldn't hand 'em over if they was rattle-snakes."

"If it comes to tradin' them two for leavin' the rest of us alone, Andy, I think it'll be a good trade. We got some family men with us. You want to be the one to tell folks how they got killed?"

Charley's remark settled nothing for the blacksmith. He walked in the direction of the creek.

Jed spoke quietly. "He's right about one thing, Charley. For takin' a shot at one of 'em . . . an' for a good reason from what I hear . . . them Injuns'll torture Shokely and Smith, or whatever their real names are, and make 'em both wish they'd never been born."

"You want an Injun war, Jed? We're down in a cañon. They'll be above us. Someone's goin' to get hurt, most likely killed. Three're dead already, from what them strangers claim."

The blacksmith was returning from the creek. He called ahead. "They're up there."

Everyone but the pair of strangers came outside, and, sure enough, there were six Indians atop the bluff, looking down into Cache Cañon.

Charley walked toward the cliff face. Where he halted, he yelled up to the hold-outs. "You want to talk? We do."

An Indian called back. "You come up here. We talk."

Several posse men muttered that it would be crazy for the constable to go up there. The butcher asked: "Ain't there enough dead men already?"

Charley went after his horse. While he was rigging out, Buck approached. Charley ignored him, but that did not discourage the younger man.

"I'll go with you," he said.

Charley looked across the seat of his saddle. "You stay here. All of you stay here."

"I know their language, Constable."

"That broncho who answered me knows our language." Charley swung astride, looking at the blacksmith. "Don't do anythin' foolhardy while I'm gone. All of you stay here."

Buck had the last word. "Stand where we can see you, then. If they take your guns, we'll come up there."

Charley crossed to the trail leading upwards and covered about half the distance when he halted to rest his hard-breathing horse. It wasn't just the posse men who were watching his progress. The original six Indians had become ten. They, too, were watching.

Charley stopped once more, near the topout, to blow his mount. The watchers below and above were like statues.

Charley reached the top and dismounted to lead his animal. Several of the Indians were weathered, older men, but the rest were young. It was the young ones who refused to nod when Charley did, but the older men nodded.

Charley tied his animal to a low, pine limb, loosened the cinch, and walked over to where the Indians were waiting. He asked which of them spoke English. Three did, but the man who had called back to Charley, a buck in his prime, said he would do the interpreting, and the others offered no objection.

Charley spoke distinctly. "My name is Charley Bent. I'm the constable from Rock City."

The dark, impassive English speaker said: "I am Man Who Hunts. These are my people." Man Who Hunts jutted his jaw, Indian fashion, to indicate one of the older men. "He is Running Horse. He is our spokesman."

Charley nodded to the older Indian, who had closely spaced, black eyes. Running Horse nodded back. Charley said: "Man Who Hunts, the man who shot at one of your people was a stranger. He and the other two came to our town about a month back."

Man Who Hunts interrupted. "Those men have been using a spyglass and making little piles of rocks in the cañon. We waited for them to go away, but they didn't. They went other places and made more little piles of rocks. We didn't want them to come up here, but they did, on foot. Their horses were left behind. We had watchers. Running Horse said to hide. To watch them, but not let them see us. Running Horse thought they would go away, but they didn't. He said if they got too close, to scare them away with bullets. We don't have many bullets, but we make balls for the old muskets. Running Horse said not to waste more than two or three bullets to scare them away. Then they got into a fight with two other white men from down below. Three white men are now dead. They shot each other. Then those two started shooting at us. We didn't want to be killed like the white men."

Man Who Hunts paused. The other Indians were watching him, particularly those who understood English. They occasionally interpreted in whispers to the others, one of whom was their spokesman. He listened without showing any expression.

Man Who Hunts gestured toward the ground. He, Running Horse, and Charley sat. The others remained standing. It would have been impossible for a white man who knew Indians to say what tribe the hold-outs belonged to. Some wore bone-hair breastplates. Some wore scraps of blue uniforms, and several had roached hair, which suggested that they might be Crows.

Charley Bent, who knew little about Indians, waited for Man Who Hunts to speak again, and eventually he did. "After some of the white men killed each other, Bear Dog showed himself. One of those white men who had been shooting fired at Bear Dog. Bear Dog is wounded, but he will not die. Those two white men ran for the cañon, where you met them and took them to the settler's old, log house. Our men split up. Most of them stayed with the wounded Bear Dog. Others chased the whiteskins. They could have shot them, but Running Horse said, no, let them go. He didn't want a fight that might bring soldiers. That was the end of it. Our young man was wounded. Three white men killed each other. What are you going to do with those two that ran away?"

Charley's answer was short. "It's up to you."

Man Who Hunts turned toward the spokesman. They conversed briefly in a language Charley could not understand.

When Man Who Hunts turned back toward Charley, he

78

said: "Running Horse said you give us the horses the white men leave behind."

Charley sighed inwardly. Because he hesitated, Man Who Hunts spoke again, more harshly this time. "For me, it would be all your horses, but Running Horse say only the three that were ridden by the men living in the settler's old, log house."

Charley's reply was tactful. "I had to think because my men want to fight. We will give you those three horses, but we will want to fetch back to town the bodies of the dead white men."

Again Man Who Hunts conferred with the spokesman, and this time the old man got up, stood beside Charley, who also rose and extended his right arm. Charley was prepared to shake hands. Running Horse gripped his arm just below the elbow, and Man Who Hunts told Charley to do the same. It would seal the bargain.

Man Who Hunts said: "One more thing we ask of you. Don't tell about us being up in here. The soldiers killed many of our people and drove the others away like cattle. We do not have many bullets, but we will defend ourselves. Do you understand?"

Charley understood and agreed, then he asked a personal question. "How's it come you speak good English?"

Man Who Hunts made a small, saturnine smile as he answered. "When I was a boy, I was one of them the soldiers drove to a reservation. I learned English from the soldiers. Some were good men. Mostly they were sons-of-bitches."

Charley grinned. Man Who Hunts had been around soldiers.

The Indians stood stoically watching Charley snug up the loose cinch on his horse, mount, and rein in the direction of the trail down. No one spoke further.

After Charley left, Running Horse asked Man Who Hunts if he trusted the whiteskin. Man Who Hunts's reply was short.

"Good man. Yes, I trust him." Then Running Horse led the Indians back among the ancient trees and passed from sight.

As Charley descended, he considered several things Man Who Hunts had said that made him think the Indians kept watch from the cliff top and probably had done so for a long time. When he reached flat ground, the posse men crowded around to ask questions as he off saddled and buckled the hobbles in place.

He told them bluntly of the trade he had made and that it insured their safety. Only one man objected. "I don't like the idea of takin' one of them strangers up to ride double with me on the way back."

Charley smiled. "They'll walk."

When the pair of strangers were told what they had to give up to stay alive, they did not seem particularly troubled. Why should they? Their mounts belonged to the liveryman in Rock City.

Charley told them: "You owe the man in town who rented you them horses. By now I'd say they was about the most expensive horses you ever rode."

It was along toward the time to eat. Charley had the two strangers remain inside the cabin. He and his riders took what supplies they wanted and went just beyond the doorway to make a small ring of stones with a fire inside it.

The butcher asked if Charley wasn't going to feed the strangers. Charley replied they could eat in good time, after everyone else was fed. He was more concerned about the ranch men who had been killed in the fight with the strangers.

Daylight ended quickly in the cañon. For the posse men who had never before encountered Indians in the vicinity of Cache Cañon, sleep would not come easily, even though Jed said he'd stand the first watch. Nor did it help when Jed yelled into the encompassing darkness that he could hear horses from the south, from the mouth of the cañon.

Every man waited wide-eyed, but the sound died away. Jed volunteered to go down the cañon, but Charley sent the blacksmith instead. When he returned an hour later to report that he had neither seen nor heard riders, Charley was relieved, but not all the posse men were.

Jed came to where the constable had unrolled the bedroll from behind his cantle. "Those were horses, Charley. I heard 'em, plain as day."

Charley continued smoothing lumps out of his bedroll as he replied: "I believe you. We all heard 'em. Want me to guess, Jed?"

"Shoot."

"It'd be the Terwilliger boys an' their riders. They told me not to come up here."

"Why?"

"Because they figure to hang the damned stranger who killed their line-shack rider, an' they got no proof who did it."

After a moment of thought, Jed had another question. "Countin' the Terwilligers, how many will there be?"

"They got three year-'round riders an' hire two more every summer. Countin' Frank and Judah P., I'd say it likely could be maybe seven, about the same as us. Get some sleep, Jed. They're not goin' to come ridin' in here when it's dark."

"Do you figure the range men that had the run-in with the strangers also came from the Terwilliger ranch?"

"Could be," conceded Charley, "or it might have been the Terwilligers themselves."

Chapter Eight

NO QUARTER

There were posse men who either had not really slept or who had slept lightly. The blacksmith had his back to the others as he coaxed a little breakfast fire to life. He did not hear riders coming from the mouth of the cañon, and, when they came into sight, there were five, heavily armed, unsmiling horsemen. Two horses were being led. Bodies were tied down across their saddles.

Lewis Boles, range boss for the Terwilligers, asked harshly: "What are you doin' around here, Constable? You were told to stay away."

Charley had finished washing at the creek and was drying his face with a large red bandanna. He looked up at the range boss. "I'll tell you, Lew, the same thing I told the Terwilligers. It's not up to you. It's up to the law to find the man you're lookin' for." He looked beyond at the bodies tied onto the horses. "Who've you got there?"

Boles snarled: "Both Frank and Judah P., as if you didn't know. We found 'em up that trail. We saw you and that posse on our way back. I'd ask you what you know about this, but I figure you already know. You got those two strangers? We found one of 'em dead up where the bosses must've had it out with 'em. This makes a heap of killin's laid against them strangers."

"We got the strangers," Charley replied evenly. "The way they tell it, Frank and Judah P. opened up on 'em. One of 'em . . . a gent named Ben Leathergood . . . is the one you

82

found where it happened. I was plannin' on headin' up there to look around this morning. We got the other two strangers in the cabin. They're both prisoners, bein' held on other charges. They claim it was self-defense in the fight with Frank and Judah P."

Boles remained silent. Charley walked over to the blanket-shrouded corpses to make an examination, first of what turned out to be Judah P.'s body, and then Frank's.

"They was shot from in front, if that's what're you're wonderin', Constable," Boles said in a hostile tone. "I got their shootin' irons here on my saddle horn. They was both fired. The way I figure it, Frank and Judah P. saw them strangers on their land, rode down on 'em while they was afoot, and the strangers opened up on 'em. There damned well better be some kinda trial for those strangers, and some quick justice."

"You know there will be, Lew," Charley assured him, although he knew there might not be. "That how you read the sign around where it happened?"

Lewis Boles dismounted. One of the other riders also swung down. There were five Terwilliger range men and seven posse men. Each group was eyeing the other. There was not a friendly look or gesture from either party.

Boles considered the posse men. He knew them. He spat aside and said: "You boys got nothin' to do with any of this. Go on home."

Jed Ames responded: "You got it wrong, Boles. We're ridin' with the law, an' you ain't."

"The Terwilligers were the law up here. It's their land, an' now they're dead . . . !"

"Their land," Jed interrupted, "ends at the mouth of the cañon."

"They claimed rights plumb up into them highlands where they was killed," Boles insisted.

Jed did not reply. He simply turned his back, and that angered the range boss further.

"You son-of-a-bitch. Do I have to knock it into your head? This is their land!"

Jed slowly faced back around, expressionless except for his eyes. He did not have Boles's quick temper, but being called a son-of-a-bitch was fight talk. "Take off that gun," Jed said, "an' try knockin' somethin' into my head."

Several posse men moved a little closer. Charley knew what was coming and knew of no way to prevent it, but he was trying his best when he addressed Boles. "I told you we got two of 'em. We'll get straight talk out of 'em, one way or another. I'm sorry about what happened between Frank, Judah P., an' them strangers, but I'll have to see a deed to the land beyond the bluff where the fight took place before I'll own the Terwilligers had any right to open up on them strangers."

Boles looked around. "How d'you know Frank and Judah P. opened up on them strangers first? An' ain't you also forgettin' them same strangers killed a Terwilliger line rider? You got 'em in that log house, Constable?"

Charley had no real opportunity to reply. Boles dropped the reins he had been holding and started in the direction of the cabin. Andy Buck stepped in front to block his way, and that was the cause of what followed.

Boles said: "Get out of my way."

Instead of answering, the blacksmith knocked Boles flat with one punch. The range boss was too dazed to get up at once, but the other riders seemed ready to back Boles's play.

A Terwilliger rider piled off his horse, crouched as he went for his six-gun, and a second Terwilliger rider, in the act of dismounting, bumped him. By the time the first rider regained his balance, three posse men had weapons in their hands which they cocked.

Stillness settled. Charley helped Lewis Boles to his feet and steadied him. There was a slight trickle of blood flung back on the range boss' mouth. He yanked free of the constable at the same time one of his men — a tall, dark, sinewy fellow — swung down and made a rush at Jed. Caught unprepared, Jed went down and dust flew. The butcher maneuvered behind this tall, dark range man and hit him over the head with his pistol barrel.

Charley's hope of preventing a brawl evaporated when another Terwilliger rider came for him, arms wide, fingers bent. Charley became too occupied to notice that it had turned into a free-for-all.

Cork Finney fought like a tiger. He downed a range man and attacked another. This time he made a mistake. Cork wasn't tall, and along with a beer belly he was out of shape. His opponent was no novice. He danced around, teased the saloonman into swinging, then stepped inside, and doubled the saloonman over with a blow that sank wrist-deep into his soft midsection. Cork went to his knees, clutching at his stomach.

A fighting posse man fell over Finney. His opponent aimed a wild kick. The posse man caught the boot and wrenched as hard as he could. The range man twisted as he fell. They both were upright in moments.

Finney gradually straightened up, but the stomach punch had hurt him. He worked his way around fighting men and entered the cabin to sit down. The strangers had heard the fighting, but without windows they could see nothing except through the open door. The bearded Bill Smith eyed Cork's holstered Colt and exchanged a look with his companion. He was tensed for the leap when a shadow obscured the open door. The town butcher's left cheek was bloody. His shirt was not only soaked with blood but hung in shreds. He leaned in the doorway, breathing from exertion, and Smith relaxed.

Outside, the brawl was continuing. Charley had his Colt out. He fired it into the air. "Hold it right there, all of you!" he yelled.

It was the first gunshot fired during the free-for-all, and it startled every man. The fighting stopped more abruptly than it had begun. Charley leathered his six-gun, looking around at the range men. None took it up again. With both their employers dead, whatever loyalty the range men felt toward the brand for which they rode was receding in the face of the posse's resistance. There was a period of stunned silence. The only onlookers — Indians in hiding — silently watched the white men again fighting each other, but they remained out of sight.

Jed rubbed his jaw, which was swelling. He turned to the range man who had struck him, yanked the six-gun from the man's holster, cocked it, and touched the range man under the ear. "Get on your god-damned horse. An' if I ever see you again, I'll slit your pouch, an' pull your leg through it. *Move!*"

The range man moved. His retreat toward the horses caused the other Terwilliger riders to follow his example. Two limped. There were several bloody faces, and one rider had a broken arm that he cradled in the other.

Charley called to Boles and the others. "Don't you think there's been enough bloodshed about land I doubt the Terwilligers owned, an' you boys don't own for sure? Any more trouble from anyone, an' I'll run in the whole pack of you. Now climb back on those horses and, for God's sake, take your bosses back to the home ranch. I'll send the coroner out from town to look over the bodies. He'll fill out the death certificates. As for the strangers, they're bein' held, an' they won't be goin' anywhere, except jail."

He was obeyed in silence, although Lewis Boles did look like he wanted to add something.

★ ★ ★ ★ ★

The sun was up, the blacksmith's little fire sent aloft a thin tendril of smoke, and Cork Finney came out of the cabin still in pain. He watched the range men going back the way they had come, leading the riderless horses with their grim burden. He watched one particular rider. It was the man who had hit him. He would never forget that range man. Adding insult to injury, when he groped in a shirt pocket for the cigar he had brought along, it was broken. He fished out the two halves, selected the longest one, lit it, and immediately began to feel better.

The posse men had certainly not emerged uninjured. The youngest among them had a bloody mouth. There were bloody shirts and bloody knuckles. They were all somewhat unnerved, including Charley, at the violence that had erupted and its consequences.

Charley watched the blacksmith limp over to his fire ring of stones and gingerly kneel to feed in more kindling. Then he went inside the cabin. Smith asked him: "What happened out there?"

When Charley told him, the bearded man smiled. "They been doggin' us like Indians."

Charley said: "Which one of you shot their line rider?"

The strangers had not come down in the last rain. They both said it was the man named Ben Leathergood, and he was dead.

Charley returned to the yard where Jed walked up with a lopsided face. "You know, Charley, in a way them old bastards had it comin'. I could stand Frank, but his brother . . . no." Jed paused briefly. "Which one of those strangers you figure killed Crittenden?"

Charley turned back toward the open door as he said: "Let's find out."

Once back inside he shouldn't have expected any answer but the one he got. "Ben Leathergood," Shokely confessed. "Snuck down there one night an' shot him."

Charley was less interested in who was lying than he was interested in something else. "Why did Leathergood shoot Crittenden?"

Al Shokely shrugged his shoulders. "Didn't like him, I guess."

Charley retorted: "You can do better'n that. Just for the hell of it, try tellin' the truth."

Shokely was dogged. "I told you. He snuck down there an' shot him."

Charley turned. This time several battered posse men were standing near the doorway. He called out to the blacksmith who gingerly entered the cabin. Charley smiled at Smith. "One last try. The truth, or Andy here'll take the pair of you an' beat the whey out of you."

Shokely got to his feet, looking at the blacksmith. Shokely was no taller, but he was a good thirty pounds heavier. Andy Buck gave look for look. He didn't appreciate what the constable had said. He hurt all over, and he'd been kicked in the kneecap, but he neither spoke nor stopped glaring at the burly man.

Charley saved his bacon when he said: "Three or four more posse men'll lend Andy a hand." The men beyond the doorway exchanged looks, arose, and crowded into the cabin. They were bruised, had bloody knuckles and torn shirts. They, too, looked stonily at Shokely.

Smith growled at Shokely: "Set down, you damned fool."

Shokely sat down, but he did it slowly and continued to stare at the blacksmith.

Charley tried again. "Which one of you shot Crittenden?"

This time Smith answered in a sullen voice and without

88

raising his head. "I don't care a damn whether you believe it or not. Leathergood went down there an' shot the storekeeper."

"Why?"

Shokely interrupted to repeat what he had said earlier. "Because he didn't like him."

Smith turned, looked at his companion, and went back to regarding the floor. "Leathergood shot him. You can't prove otherwise, because it's the truth." Smith raised his head. "You goin' to starve us?"

The aroma from the blacksmith's little cooking fire was inside the cabin, and the blacksmith pushed his way clear to return to it. Charley led the others outside. For lack of plates the blacksmith dished a kind of fragrant hash onto some of the scattered cedar shakes from the broken roof. He and the others ate like horses. Enough time had passed in this fashion for their earlier tightly bound muscles and nerves to return to normal.

Not a word was said as they ate. As one posse man threw his improvised plate away, he asked Andy what he had made the hash out of. Andy asked if the speaker had liked it. When the man nodded his head, the blacksmith went back to tending his fire without saying any more.

They didn't feed the strangers until they were finished, and Charley and Jed had ridden off with one of the posse men's horses to look over the scene of the shoot-out with the Terwilligers and bring in Ben Leathergood's body.

When Charley and Jed returned, with Leathergood's body wrapped in a blanket and tied onto the saddle of the spare horse, the constable told the posse members that, from all appearances, there was nothing to contradict the account of what had happened given by the remaining two strangers, and confirmed by the Indians, that the Terwilligers had opened up and got themselves killed in the ensuing gun play. Jed backed up what Charley said.

The constable then walked to the cabin and through the doorway. He said to the prisoners: "On your feet."

Both Shokely and Smith stood up. Charley moved aside for them to pass out of the cabin. The posse men were all mounted, one doubling up with the butcher. Jed was holding Charley's reins.

Shokely stopped dead still. "What about horses for us?"

Charley answered curtly. "Remember? I gave 'em to the Injuns to buy our way out of here. Your henchman is already on one of our horses."

"Well, then, ain't we goin' to ride double?" Shokely asked.

Charley jerked his head and said: "Start walkin'." He went to take the reins to his horse. The pair of strangers had come to stand like statues until Charley called from the saddle: "Walk ahead of us."

This time it was Bill Smith who spoke. "Walk, for Christ's sake?"

"All the way back to town. Now, start."

Shokely and Smith proceeded out of Cache Cañon with the posse men behind them. The horse Cork Finney was riding was not only a fast walker but yanked at the reins when Cork tried to make him walk slower.

The posse men with their prisoners weren't very long out of the cañon before Indians appeared from hiding. They scavenged the camp. There was little to scavenge until they found the supplies. These they appropriated down to the last tin.

It was hot in open country. The men on foot guessed the shortest distance to Rock City and adhered to it. There was little conversation among the posse men. Their injuries were beginning to hurt. The posse rider with the bloody mouth had to grit his teeth. He was white to the hairline, but, when one of the others commiserated, the injured man growled. There was nothing anyone could do that would really help him. Each step his horse took shot pain through his body.

At this point in a low voice Jed told Charley he doubted whether the seriously injured man could ride the full distance, and the constable, who had watched the man with the torn and bleeding mouth, replied in an equally quiet voice: "When he gets too bad off, we'll leave him in the shade somewhere and come back for him with a buggy."

And that is what they did. The posseman fell from his horse when they had covered about half the distance. He fortunately did not land on his face, but he was dazed by the fall. When Charley leaned over him, he looked up with a blank stare and said: "I don't think I want to ride any more."

They found a gully where there were trees, made him as comfortable as they could, and left him. He fainted minutes after he was left behind.

The heat increased. The walking men sweated, but they were tough individuals. They only stopped when a posseman offered them his canteen, which they nearly drained, then resumed their way. Neither of them would look back until Cork's horse got cranky, lunged to get less pressure on the restraining reins, and stepped on Smith's heel. Smith swore but kept on walking. Charley told the saloonman to get behind the last horse and stick his mount's nose as close to the horse ahead as he could. It worked. The high-strung animal settled down.

When they finally halted near a warm-water creek to tank up the horses, Shokely and Smith continued to walk. Jed yelled at them to come back, which they did, got belly down, and drank deeply from the creek. Afterward, they sat in the shade of a creek-willow a short distance from the posse men. They occasionally spoke to each other.

When the ride resumed, Andy Buck shook his head about the prisoners, but said nothing. It had been a long walk under an unfriendly sun. The blacksmith did not have to like the strangers, but now he sure as hell respected them.

Once they saw four horsemen, watching from a good distance, and Jed made a guess. "What'll they do now that Judah P. and Frank are dead?"

Charley didn't answer. He was standing in his stirrups, looking for rooftops. He saw them, but they weren't close, and directly daylight would fade. They finally did make it to town as the first shadows of dusk arrived. It was suppertime. The main street was empty on both sides as they rode as far as the jailhouse. Charley locked his prisoners inside and returned to the street to walk with his horse to the livery barn. The hosteler was there. Jim Neely was over at the café. The hosteler watched the posse men ride up with wide eyes and an open mouth, but, as he was helping with the off saddling, he was wise enough not to ask any of the questions he dearly would have liked to ask.

Cork Finney told the hosteler to rig out a light buggy. Cork was still waiting as the posse riders went their separate ways.

Charley and Jed went back up to the jailhouse. As they were entering, Jed said: "I'm hungrier'n a bitch wolf."

Charley was, too, but he said: "Go get fed."

Jed shook his head. "Later. Right now I want to hear those buzzards sing."

Charley brought Shokely and Smith into the office. They looked exhausted, and were. They sat together on the same bench, stonily regarding the constable and the harness maker.

Charley asked his first question. "What were you doin' up yonder? Surveying?"

Shokely answered. "Studyin' the country. Is that against the law?"

92

Charley was as tired as the strangers were, but it went deeper, because he was older. He sat at his desk, thumbed back his hat, gazing at the men on the bench. "What did them little piles of rocks mean?"

As before it was Al Shokely who answered, but he took a circuitous way of doing it. "Ben Leathergood was the surveyor. We did what he told us. Now them damned Terwilligers killed him. . . ." Shokely leaned with both elbows on his legs. "Neither of us know how to use that spyglass of his on its tripod." The man sounded dejected.

Charley tried again. "What were you doin' up there?"

This time it was Bill Smith who answered. There was no mistaking his bitterness when he said: "There's a fortune up there somewhere."

Charley looked disgusted. "You mean a cache?"

"Yes."

"Hell," Charley said, "that fable's been around longer'n I have."

Jed was nodding his head when Smith spoke with spirit. "Fable, your butt. It's up there. Shokely an' me got a map. Leathergood pitched in with us to find it. He had the savvy. We had the map."

Charley hitched a little in the chair before speaking. "Mister, folks've been diggin' holes like prairie dogs all over that foothill country. They been doin' that since I come to this country, an' all they've come up with is old Injun clay pots an' such like."

"Then tell me why that draw up yonder is called Cache Cañon?" Smith retorted.

Charley's stomach thought his throat had been cut. He herded the strangers back to their strap-steel cage, locked them in, and returned to the office where he tossed the key on the desk. He jerked his head for Jed to follow him over to the café.

On the way Jed asked: "Why *do* folks call that draw Cache Cañon?"

Charley was too tired and disgusted to answer, but that didn't deter the harness maker.

"Smith said they got a map, Charley."

The constable paused as he opened the café door. "Every cache-hunter's got a map."

As Jed followed Charley toward the counter, he commented: "An' you didn't believe there was Injuns up there."

Chapter Nine

FITTING PIECES TOGETHER

As he sat in his office alone after supper, Charley toyed with an idea. He was pretty long in the tooth to change, and a man gray as a badger couldn't alter a lifelong conviction quickly. The constable would have trouble changing. But the more he sat thinking about it, the more convinced he became that it was true. If he wanted the truth, he might *starve* it out of his prisoners. Of course, it wasn't something the law would condone, but Charley remembered something Frank Terwilliger had said. There was no comparison between justice and the law. Charley Bent wouldn't be the only man to reach that same conclusion.

He was still sitting at the desk when waspish Sam Brennen came in. "I heard you brought in two of them strangers."

Charley considered the small, nervous man, leaned back, and replied testily: "That's right, but, as far as I know, they didn't stop your coach."

Once again the corral-yard boss's temper flared. "As far as *you* know," he repeated sarcastically. "As far as *I* know, Charley, an' from the talk goin' around . . . there's three of 'em."

"One of 'em . . . a feller known as Ben Leathergood . . . is dead. He was killed by the Terwilligers."

That drove Brennen to a chair. "Yes, I know. I heard about that. It was a terrible thing to have happened."

"It was."

"But . . . before that one got shot . . . it could have been the three of them, couldn't it, Charley?"

The constable stood up and moved toward the center of the room to take down the lamp. While holding the mantle of the lamp, he said: "It's been a hell of a day, Sam. Good night." Then he blew it out.

Brennen got up to leave in the darkness. "Well, then, good night, Charley."

Following Brennen's departure, Charley hung the lamp back on its hook and locked the jailhouse after himself. He went up as far as the harness shop where Jed was at his cutting table with two lamps brightening the shop. Charley hesitated and then entered.

Jed looked up, sighed, and wiped both hands before offering coffee which the constable declined as he came forward and sank into a chair.

Jed cocked his head slightly. "You look like you been pulled through a knothole."

"I feel like it," the constable replied, and told the harness maker about Sam Brennen's visit.

Jed got himself a cup of coffee from the pot atop the stove. He went to lean on the counter. "I do a lot of work for Sam, but I can't take more'n half an hour of his company."

"He wanted to know if Leathergood an' those other two strangers were the ones who held up the stage."

"Did you tell him how Leathergood got killed?"

"He already knew about it," Charley said, and looked across the room at the harness maker. "I was tired. I've never much cared for him, either. I got rid of him, but I can tell you one thing. By morning it'll be all over town, an' most likely he'll claim those strangers were in on the hold-up. As it stands, I can't prove it one way or the other."

Jed Ames was a practical man. "So it'll spread around town, anyway, just like it has about the Terwilligers. They have friends in this town. And, after all, we did come back with two of the strangers."

"I don't plan to tell Brennen about the hold-outs."

"Charley, you probably won't have to. By now that's got spread around, too. There just wasn't no way to prevent it. We all saw them Injuns."

Charley changed his mind, got a cup of coffee, and returned to his chair. He thought of old Running Horse and the big broncho he'd palavered with. What Jed had said was a fact. Even if he'd sworn the posse men from town to an oath not to mention the Indians, it was too good a secret not to be told.

Charley sipped coffee as black as the bottom of a well. "I promised Man Who Hunts, the Injun I talked to, I wouldn't say a word about 'em bein' up there, Jed."

The harness maker surprised the constable. "Like I just said, Charley, there's no way under the sun it's not goin' to get around. But I got an idea. What do they want most up there?"

"Bullets, I suppose. Man Who Hunts said they didn't have many."

"Suppose I ride up there tomorrow, give 'em some cartons of bullets, an' explain to 'em that, while you'll never break your word, the rest of us saw 'em. I'll tell 'em to go farther into the high country an' brush out their sign. If they see riders comin', it's best they should hide."

Charley put his unfinished cup of coffee on the counter. "That's a long ride, Jed, an' you never can tell about Injuns."

"I'll leave in the dark tomorrow mornin'."

Charley stood, considering the coffee cup. Eventually he said: "You're a good man."

After he left the shop, he went to his quarters at the hotel. He slept like a dead man.

The sun was up before Charley went to the café and, afterward, he rattled the street door of the harness shop. It was locked.

Down at the jailhouse he took a bucket of drinking water to Shokely and Smith, leaned outside the cage, and asked a question. "Where's the map?"

Smith answered because Shokely was using the dipper to drink from the bucket. "Leathergood had it. He used it for sightin' with his surveyin' instrument."

Shokely finished drinking, dragged a filthy cuff across his mouth, and looked defiantly at the constable. "Somethin' I learned years ago. A town constable's authority don't extend beyond his town. Only a sheriff, or maybe a federal lawman, can lock folks up he's caught away from a town."

Charley's attention shifted to the burly man. His gaze was cold. "I can guess how you found that out. Somethin' else you don't know is that, when a lawman's the only peace officer for a good many miles, his job ain't limited to town."

He returned to the office and was about to slam the intervening door between the office and the cell room when Shokely called to him. "You goin' to feed us? You walked our butts off yesterday, an' we ain't been fed since before leavin' that damned cañon."

"Live off your fat," Charley advised, then he closed the door.

Cork came down from the saloon. He had accompanied Dr. Reese out to see the injured posse man. After attending to the man, the doctor had gone on to the Terwilliger ranch. Cork had brought the posse man back to town in a wagon.

Charley did not mention the harness maker nor his mission, but Cork said the talk around town was about the hold-outs. Charley commented that he couldn't hold Smith and Shokely indefinitely.

98

Cork's retort was stern: "Let us know when you're going to turn 'em out."

Raymond Kemp appeared in the jailhouse doorway to ask if Charley had brought up to Al Shokely anything about that scrap of a newspaper article. Charley hadn't and said so. Because the constable seemed to be in a bad mood, the hotelman left.

By mid-afternoon the men in the cell room were demanding loudly to be fed. They also cursed the constable, which rolled off him easily. What did get his attention was when Jed Ames returned after dark, tired and hungry, to put someone's half stiff bandanna on the lawman's desk. He sat down and said he'd met with the broncho named Man Who Hunts who had given him the bandanna, and that the Indian had listened to what Jed had to say about moving deeper into the badlands and leaving no tracks. Man Who Hunts had agreed. When Jed put the cartons of ammunition on the ground between them, Man Who Hunts had asked Jed to tell the constable the Indians thought he was a good man, for someone with a white skin, and that they would welcome him back in their territory.

While Jed was talking, Charley untied the bandanna. It contained a sizable packet of greenbacks along with other things a man would carry in his pockets, such as a large, sharp-bladed clasp knife, some coins, a chewed pencil, and a folded scrap of paper Charley spread flat as Jed finished talking.

"They scavenged the camp of those strangers," Jed explained. "That's where they got some of that stuff. The money and the map they got off Leathergood's body before we went up to fetch it back."

Charley leaned close to study the map. It was expertly drawn of the country northwest of Rock City. There was no writing, but Charley had no difficulty following the lines to Cache Cañon.

Jed got up, and Charley moved a lamp closer so they could study it. They were engrossed in this when a faded Lewis Boles walked in, smelling powerfully of a visit to Cork Finney's establishment. The unshaven and unwashed Terwilliger range boss went directly to the constable's desk. He handed Charley an envelope.

Jed whisked away the map as Charley removed a piece of paper from the envelope. He started to read it, looked up once at Boles, then resumed his reading. When he finished, he put the paper and its envelope aside.

"I didn't know Frank an' Judah P. had kin."

Boles nodded. "It wasn't somethin' that got talked much about. It's Frank's kid. Lived up in Cheyenne with the mother. That's all I ever gleaned in all the years I worked for 'em. I expect now it won't be much of a secret. The names ain't the same, Constable. The name mentioned in that will is Thatcher . . . A. Thatcher."

Boles paused. When Charley said nothing, he asked if the constable thought he should write up to Cheyenne and say both Frank and Judah P. were dead, or did he want to do it. The way Boles phrased himself made it clear he did not want to write the letter, not because he disliked the notion of writing that kind of letter, but because he did not know how to write.

Charley agreed to take care of it. Boles said Dr. Reese had been out to the ranch, and that he and the other ranch hands had buried the bodies on a small hill behind the ranch house. He then asked if Charley thought he and the others should stay on, pending the arrival of the heir, because, if he did advise that, he ought to know the men were due to be paid shortly.

Charley's answer was careful. He hadn't known there was an heir before Lewis Boles had walked in. He had no way of

100

knowing whether the heir would come to Rock City or whether the men would be paid. "It's up to you fellers. But if you leave, most likely you won't get paid."

Lewis Boles would have retrieved the Terwilliger will, but Charley stopped him. "I'll need it for the address up in Cheyenne."

"O.K., Constable," Boles conceded, and then gave Charley a hard stare. "Expect you'll be bringin' those strangers to trial for murderin' the Terwilligers soon as the circuit judge gets here."

"Expect so," Charley lied, and nodded at Boles as he turned to leave.

Once the Terwilliger range boss was out of earshot, Jed said: "I wouldn't have your job for ten thousand dollars."

Charley grinned. "I wouldn't, neither." He returned to studying the map.

Finally Jed left. He was not only saddle sore, he was hungry, and the cranky proprietor of the café sometimes closed early.

Charley used a magnifying glass. For some years he'd had trouble seeing things clearly up close. He'd been told by George Crittenden, among others, to see one of those eye doctors up in Denver City and get fitted with glasses, but Charley considered that as something he would not admit to others or to himself, so he used a magnifying glass for seeing clearly up close.

It was while he was concentrating on the map that he had another unexpected visitor. The nondescript clerk from the Emporium came in, apologized for arriving so late and put the constable's mail on Charley's desk. The top letter looked official and important, which is why the clerk thought he had better deliver it since Charley hadn't been in to pick it up. Having said that, he left.

Charley opened the official letter and ignored the other

two. He held in his hand a copy of an extradition paper, signed by the governor, and a short letter from a lawman, Cliff Given, down in Brownsville, Texas. Charley was now authorized to send one of the strangers — Bill Morgan — to Brownsville.

He leaned back, put the magnifying glass in the drawer in case he might have any more inadvertent visitors, leaned back, and rubbed his eyes.

It was too late to bring Smith out to the office. He would do that first thing in the morning. He left the papers atop his desk, blew out the lamp, locked the jailhouse from the outside, and went to the hotel.

Sleep did not come easily this night. For one thing, he'd never heard of either of the Terwilligers having kin. If it had been known in Cache Valley that Frank had had an illegitimate child, he surely would have heard. That was the kind of gossip people thrived on. His thoughts were less concerned with the extradition order. He would be glad to get rid of the bank robber.

After breakfast in the morning, Charley went to the jailhouse, brought the bearded man to his office, and without speaking handed Smith the extradition order. Smith studied it a long time before handing it back and raising his gaze to the constable.

"How'd they know?" he asked.

Charley evaded a direct answer by asking a question of his own. "Your name was Morgan then?"

Instead of replying, the bearded man said: "They can't do nothin', Constable. They can't prove it was me."

Charley gently inclined his head. "They can prove it was you. There was a witness."

Smith scowled. "Son-of-a-bitch! I thought I'd seen that

feller before. Couldn't remember where."

"What feller?"

"That damned blacksmith."

Charley smiled thinly. "You as well as admitted you robbed that bank. Get up."

Charley herded the bearded man back to his cage and locked him in. Then he took Al Shokely back to the front office with him, told him to sit down, and went behind his desk. He was leaning forward when he asked: "Why would a man carry a newspaper clippin' around with him that said he killed a man, his wife, an' little girl?"

Shokely's gaze went swiftly to the wall beyond the desk and back. "I got no idea what you're talkin' about."

Charley got slowly to his feet and started around the desk. Shokely stood up. Charley grabbed him by the shirt and slammed him against the wall. "A little girl, you no-good bastard."

Shokely's eyes bulged, but he made no move to raise his arms to protect himself. He said: "What in hell are you talkin' about?"

Charley yanked him forward and slammed him harder against the wall.

Shokely squawked. "You can't touch me. That's the law."

Charley jerked Shokely forward and slammed him back in the chair. "I'm not goin' to touch you. I'm goin' to tell it around town that you shot a woman an' a little girl. Then I'm goin' to ride out of town. When they drag you out of here an' hang you, mister, they'll overhaul you until you can't stand alone. Killin' the man was bad enough, but killin' the woman . . . an' the little girl . . . ! When I come back, there'll be somethin' left at the end of a rope your mother wouldn't recognize."

Shokely said nothing for a long time. He got white. Then

103

he spoke. "He wasn't no saint. One of the folks on one of them stages we held up said he'd show us how to get rich for not shootin' him. He give us a map, showin' where a treasure was buried. We had to ride to his stump ranch with him to get it."

"Who was *we?*"

"Ben Leathergood an' me. The fellow got the map, handed it up to Ben. His wife an' little girl come out onto the porch. Ben handed me the map and drew his six-gun. He shot all three of 'em."

Charley leaned back. "Leathergood shot 'em?"

"Yes."

"But you was carryin' the newspaper clippin'."

It was a shot in the dark. Charley had no idea who had been carrying the clipping.

Shokely's gaze jumped past Charley and then back. "He didn't want folks to know he was carryin' it."

Charley did not blink during a long moment before he spoke again. "You're a lyin' son-of-a-bitch. The clipping said folks saw one man ride to the stump ranch. They heard gunshots, an' saw one man ride away."

This time Charley's ruse didn't work. Shokely looked straight at the constable as he spoke. "There wasn't no one saw anythin'. Where them folks lived was in a grove of trees without no neighbors for miles."

"A grove of trees miles from any neighbor?"

"Yes."

"How would you know that unless you was there?"

"I never said I wasn't there. It was Ben an' me together."

"I think you're a damned liar."

"Prove it, Constable."

"One stranger rode in, an' one stranger rode away afterwards."

"Prove that, too," Shokely said. He was sweating and nervous.

Charley returned Shokely to his cell, went back to sit at his desk, and was still sitting there when Ray Kemp walked in. Charley was irritated but tried not to show it. It was Kemp who had opened this whole damned can of worms.

As Kemp sat, Charley said: "There were three strangers. One got himself killed up yonder, and one I got an extradition order for bank robbin'. That leaves Al Shokely, the one who murdered that feller, his wife, an' little girl."

Kemp made a wide smile. "You got 'em all tagged, then."

Charley glared. "I can't prove a damned thing against Shokely."

Kemp got up, hitched his way to the desk, and tossed something on the surface of it. "There's the other part of that clippin'," he said.

Charley spread out the crumpled scrap of newspaper very carefully. "Where did you get this?"

Kemp did not answer until Charley had finished reading the torn piece of paper and had brought forth the other clipping, placing them together. They fit perfectly. The topmost piece of paper gave a date and the legend in bold black letters. **THE BOZEMAN MONTANA STAR AND TELEGRAPH**.

When Charley looked at him, Kemp said: "After the last time we talked, I went through the rubbish I cleaned out of the rooms after they vamoosed without paying. This piece was rolled into a ball that I took to be a sock or maybe a handkerchief. What tipped me off was the big black letters." Kemp was clearly pleased with himself. "Now all you got to do is write up there for the whole damned story."

Charley's gloomy mood before Kemp had arrived vanished. He thanked the hotelman. He would write up to Montana to learn if a warrant had been issued and hope very hard the folks

105

up there would answer promptly.

He had never in all his years as a lawman wanted to get a man hanged as much as he now wanted that to happen to Shokely.

Chapter Ten

A DECEPTIVE TIME

Charley wrote the letter to Montana and got a surprise when he crossed to the Emporium to mail it. The clerk was dusting shelves. The person who took Charley's letter to be posted was a woman — not just any woman, but a female with biceps like a blacksmith and pale eyes that looked right through a person.

Her name was Bertha Crittenden. She was George Crittenden's only living relative and was, therefore, his heir. She introduced herself and shook Charley's hand with a grip that would thaw hard ice.

On his way back to the jailhouse Charley told himself the world was changing. Women didn't usually own general stores, and especially ones built like a brick wall and with a grip from which the constable's fingers were still tingling.

His prisoners were dragging tin cups across their cages. Charley took his time about going down to stand outside their cells and wait until their threats of retaliation for starving them had subsided, then he said he would fetch them grub when they told the truth. Smith said in a desperate voice that he had told the truth. Charley's gaze swung to Shokely. They looked steadily at each other for some time. Neither of them said a word.

Charley went back up front and barred the cell-room door from the office side. He stood listening until he heard the argument start, then he went over to the café, got two trays of food, and returned to the office where he placed the trays on his desk, then brought Smith in to eat. While he was eating,

Charley asked him about the argument.

Speaking around a mouthful of food, Smith said: "The son-of-a-bitch said he told you the truth, an' he's a damned liar. Me 'n' Leathergood knew about that shootin' of them stump ranchers. Shokely told us one night in camp when we was on our way down to Rock City. He showed us part of a newspaper about it."

"Why in hell would a man in his right mind carry somethin' like that around with him?" Charley asked, and got another answer around a mouthful of food.

"I sure as hell wouldn't, an' neither would Leathergood, but Shokely said, if he hadn't shot 'em, we wouldn't have got the map. He was right about that, I guess." Smith paused to swallow. He looked balefully at Charley. "You want to know who shot the storekeeper? It was Shokely. You want to know why? Because the night it happened, Leathergood told us he knew within a few yards where the cache was, an' Shokely rode away after dark. In the mornin', while we was eatin', he told us he didn't see no reason why we should give a share to old 'possum belly. He said he'd rode down here and shot him."

Smith refilled his mouth, swallowed, and continued. "Me 'n' Leathergood agreed. There wasn't no reason to share the cache, an' that ended it."

Charley watched Smith wolf down the food. In his lengthy career as a lawman he couldn't recall ever running across such cold-blooded killers as these strangers. What he said to the prisoner, as he scarfed up every scrap, was simply that Leathergood's death had provided them both with an excuse for blaming leathergood for everything. smith did not comment, except to say that the Terwilligers started shooting as they rode down on them, and that what shooting he and Shokely had done was in self-defense.

When Charley returned Smith to his cell, he brought the

burly Shokely out to the office. Shokely didn't have to be told to eat. He shoved Smith's empty platter aside, sat down, and began. Charley was in no hurry. He did not open the conversation until Shokely had finished half the food. Then he said: "Where did you find Leathergood?"

"Up north. He was down on his luck."

"He was a real surveyor?"

"Yep. Me 'n' Bill talked it over. We made him an offer of a share of the cache. I expect, because he had nothin' to lose, he threw in with us."

"Did he figure out where the cache was?"

"He said it had to be within the upper part of the eastern slope. He couldn't place it any closer'n that. He knew how to work that three-legged telescope he had. I think, given a few more days, he'd have figured the exact location."

"Why did the three of you go up into the country behind the cañon?"

"To poke around." Shokely paused to swallow before looking at the constable. "If we'd knowed that we'd have a run-in with those ranchers, we wouldn't have gone. The one that Leathergood shot was practically on top of us, firing his six-gun. The other rancher finished Leathergood. I don't know whose shot finished him, mine or Bill's. It was either shoot back or get killed, standin' there. Then one of those tomahawks come from behind some rocks. He was raisin' an old musket. I admit I fired at him. I think I hit him, but not too bad. It was my last bullet. Bill and I started off at a run, an' kept goin' till we run into you and the posse. We figured on forting up in the cabin and holdin' off the tomahawks."

"How'd you happen to be up there on foot?"

"We'd been usin' the horses hard the last few days. We rode a ways, left the horses staked out, and hiked the rest of the way. It was just plain curiosity."

Charley leaned forward, fixed the torn newspaper so that the parts fitted, and told Al Shokely to have a close look. When Shokely did and saw the reassembled newspaper page, he let go a long breath, staring blankly at the constable. "Where'd that come from?" he asked.

Charley told him.

Shokely ran a hand over his stubbly jaw. "What about it?"

"You tell me."

"It's just some pieces from an old newspaper. Like I said before, I. . . ."

"I know what you said before," Charley interrupted. "You said you 'n' Leathergood rode to the stump ranch, an' he shot the man, his wife, an' the little girl. Leathergood didn't make that ride. You made it alone."

With the pleats out of his stomach, Shokely looked stonily at the constable. "Ben went with me," he reiterated.

"Bill Smith said you went alone. He said you told him an' Ben Leathergood what you did."

"Bill's a damned liar!"

"Why did you carry that clippin' from the newspaper around with you?"

"I didn't. Leathergood carried it."

Charley decided he'd made a mistake. He should have questioned Al Shokely before allowing him to eat. He rose and jerked his head.

As before, after he returned to the office from locking Shokely in, he leaned against the cell-room door. Another argument erupted. While Charley could distinguish the loudest words, he could not make out much more. Nonetheless, he was satisfied. He had done it before, encouraged prisoners to argue among themselves.

He returned the empty platters to the caféman and went up to the harness shop where Jed Ames had a piece of skirting

110

leather clamped between the jaws of his sewing horse and was punching holes with an awl before inserting the two needles. Jed looked up. He had never liked the sewing part of his work. Almost any excuse was good enough to make him quit. He eased back on the seat of his sewing horse.

"How're you makin' out?" he asked, and got the first faint grin he'd seen on Charley Bent's face in days.

"I'll get rid of that Bill Smith as soon as there's a southbound stage. The other one . . . Shokely . . . is sure as hell wanted in Montana for three murders. Maybe more. But the extradition business's got to be gone through first, an' that'll take time."

Jed had a question. "You seen the woman who inherited George's store? She's big enough to chew nails an' spit rust. Charley . . . ?"

"What."

"She ain't married."

"Why tell me?"

"You ain't married, neither."

The constable leaned on the counter as he replied: "Neither are you. She's stout enough to sew traces and skirts all day."

Jed changed the subject. "Jim Neely come up for some halters. He said he was lookin' for you." Jed grinned. "About them three horses you let the hold-outs keep."

Charley got himself a cup of coffee and returned to the counter. "I'll pay him for 'em."

"They may be worth a fortune," Jed warned.

Charley nodded solemnly, drained the cup, and went back out into the autumn sunshine, which was as bright as ever but with less heat.

Across the road there were four horses at Finney's Pleasure Palace tie rack, wearing McClellen saddles with blue blanket rolls behind each cantle. Charley went over for a closer look.

The bridles were also Army issue and the S-shaped bits had small brass circles with U S stamped on each side of the bits.

Charley stood a moment, gazing at the saloon's dual spindle doors, then pushed his way inside. The four soldiers — two officers and two sergeants — were being served at the bar. When Cork saw the constable enter, he got busy refilling little jolt glasses and said loudly: "It's just talk. I been here more years than I like to think about, an' the rumors've been around that long. But I can tell you for a fact, I've rode over a lot of country without seein' an Indian nor any sign of 'em."

Charley might have smiled any other time. Cork had done well at alerting the constable concerning the purpose of soldiers' visit to Rock City. The constable approached the bar, nodded, and waited for Cork to put up the bottle and little glass. They exchanged a blank look before Cork moved on.

One of the blue uniforms, a captain by his shoulder insignias, considered Charley's badge briefly, then asked if Charley knew anything about hold-outs in the primitive country to the north. Charley lied without allowing his gaze to move from the soldier.

"Talk. Folks been seein' Injuns up there since before I come here. You listen long enough, an' you'll be told some of the dangedest lies you'll ever hear."

The captain asked if Charley knew the uplands.

Charley's response was truthful — as far as it went. "I just come back from up there, lookin' for some horses the liveryman lost. That's rough country, Captain. Rocks bigger'n a mounted man, fir trees bigger around than a rain barrel. Bears, cougars, wolves. They routed out the Injuns years ago. If you go up there, all you'll find is where they was . . . old camps, maybe old grave platforms . . . but you won't find no Injuns. Mind if I ask where you got the information there was hold-outs up there?"

"From a stage passenger who got robbed some weeks back. He said he'd take an oath the three highwaymen was Indians."

Charley snorted. "They wasn't Indians. I got two of 'em in the jailhouse. The other one got shot. It's them, sure as hell. They haven't confessed yet, but they will."

A grizzled sergeant built like a Durham bull, red-faced and red-haired, sounded disgusted when he addressed the captain. "I told you. I was with the Army when we made a sweep of this country. We didn't miss any."

The officer reddened and reached for his jolt glass. The sergeant was an old campaigner. His kind spoke up to officers. Lesser enlisted men didn't, unless they wanted stockade time.

The smooth-faced lieutenant ignored the jolt glass in front of him to address Charley. "How about the outlying cow outfits? Wouldn't they know if there were Indians in the mountains?"

This time it was Cork Finney who saved Charley from expanding on his prevarication. Cork said: "Mister, I talk to 'em all right here at my bar. I can tell you for a fact I ain't heard no talk of Indians bein' seen since I come to Rock City."

It was, in its own way, a magnificent lie, and it was stated without a blink. Afterwards, Charley chided Cork about it and was told blandly: "My father said to me, when I wasn't much more'n a button, the Irish are some of the best liars in the world. The English made us that way."

The soldiers went out to stand on the plank walk, gazing to the northwest. Even at that distance the highlands looked darkly forbidding. The sergeant addressed his captain again. "These horses have had about all they can stand. It's one more of them old wives' tales."

The soldiers mounted and rode southward. People saw them, and some of the men folk went up to the saloon, which was good for Cork's business. He retold the story for several

113

days until it no longer enticed customers.

Charley mentioned the soldiers to Jed. The harness maker rolled his eyes without comment.

It was an unpleasant duty the constable had to perform. He went to the corral yard to tell Sam Brennen he had a prisoner to be transported southward.

"He'll be in chains," Charley said. "Your gun guard can keep an eye on him."

Sam gave the constable one of his sulphurous looks. "The company don't pay its gun guards to do the law's business."

"You'll get paid," Charley stated flatly.

That earned a waspish reply. "Where's he goin'?"

"To Brownsville, Texas."

"Hah! I'll get one of them Texas vouchers that take a year to collect."

Charley didn't relent. "There's no other way, or I'd use it. I'll have him up here in chains for the morning coach tomorrow."

"What's his name?"

"Calls himself Bill Smith. In Brownsville, where he robbed a bank, he called himself Morgan."

"One of them strangers?" When Charley nodded, the corral-yard boss got red in the face. "Damned stage robber."

Charley turned and, saying no more, left the corral-yard office.

When he got back to the jailhouse, he brought Smith into the office and asked him about the stage robbery.

Smith did not deny it. He said: "We was runnin' short of money."

Charley told Smith he was going to ride the morning stage in chains on his way back to Brownsville, and the bearded man sat a long moment before speaking.

114

"How about Shokely?"

"When I get the extradition papers, he's goin' back to Montana. They'll likely hang him."

Smith smiled. "He's a cold-blooded son-of-a-bitch, Constable."

Charley put Smith back in his cage. Smith's final remark about Al Shokely had come as no surprise. In fact, of his two prisoners, Al Shokely was the one Charley thoroughly detested.

Next he sent off the letter to Frank Terwilliger's heir up in Cheyenne and forgot about it. He sat in the jailhouse office and relaxed for the first time in weeks. All he had to do now was ship Bill Smith to Texas and wait for the papers of extradition for Al Shokely. He wasn't pleased about the killings in Cache Cañon. In all honesty he had come to feel a deep remorse over the passing of the Terwilliger brothers. However contentious they had been, they also had been a part of the community for a long time.

He got a pair of leg irons from a small, cluttered storeroom, oiled them, and tossed them aside. Later he brought two platters from the café and left them with his prisoners. There was not a word said as he did this. Smith and Shokely were both surly.

Up at Cork Finney's place, where Charley went after supper, there were several local range men. They did not speak, but they eyed the constable with one part wonder and one part respect. Cork stood the first round and broke a saloonman's rule: he had a drink with the constable. Charley told him Smith would be sent to Texas in irons the following morning, and Cork refilled their glasses about that, then changed the subject.

"You met that cousin or somethin' that inherited the Emporium?"

Charley nodded. "I hear she's single, Cork."

The saloonman stared, then wagged his head. "Bein' single's

115

got advantages. I never been that hard up, Charley. How about you?"

Charley smiled.

There was a chill in the night air. Autumn was passing. Up at the hotel Raymond Kemp was lurking. When Charley entered, Kemp asked: "The strangers found it, did they?"

"Found what?"

"That cache folks've been huntin' over the years."

"If they did," Charley replied dryly, "it's not goin' to do 'em any good. That's another damned myth. I've been other places where there's stories of a cache. I figured it was pure bull then, an' I believe it's pure bull now. Good night."

Charley had to be down at the jailhouse at sunrise. That was when the southbound stage left Rock City. He had to hurry. Sam Brennen wouldn't delay a scheduled departure even for the angel, Gabriel.

Bill Smith was an unco-operative individual this morning. He complained about missing breakfast but stoically accepted the leg and wrist irons. The sun was beginning to show off in the chilly east when Charley delivered his prisoner to the corral yard, braced for Brennen's displeasure. Sam eyed the filthy, surly man in irons and sneered.

"Good riddance," he said, and left it to Charley to help Smith into the coach.

Smith looked balefully out at the corral-yard boss, but said nothing. There were only two other passengers, both men. One had a belted six-gun showing. The other passenger was a drummer who wore a curly brimmed derby and matching trousers and coat. He moved as far as he could from the prisoner.

The other passenger showed no expression as he regarded

116

the prisoner, until Smith eyed his sidearm, then the gun's owner said: "You try it, mister, an' I'll bust you wide open."

Charley gave the keys to the prisoner's hand and leg irons to the gun guard and then joined Sam Brennen where he stood. Together they watched the stage and four make a wide sashay into the roadway and head south through town at a dead walk. Sam Brennen was neither the worst nor the best employer, but one of his rules was that horses were to be walked a full mile to warm up before being boosted into a faster gait.

Brennen said: "How about the other one?"

Charley replied curtly: "Not yet." He dug into a pocket and pulled out the greenbacks Jed had brought back from his council with the hold-outs. "This money was found on Leathergood's body. Apparently he acted as the banker for those strangers. It should be enough to cover the claims of those passengers."

Brennen was too surprised and pleased to be angry over any perceived delay there had been in the return of the money. "You got 'em with the goods, then?" He took the proferred greenbacks.

"Smith, or Morgan, admits to the robbery. Shokely admits to robbin' stages, but not yours. I hope we can prove it in court, but now Smith's gone to face a more serious charge. Shokely, too, may be wanted on a more serious charge than stage robbery."

"I know," Brennen said fiercely. "I've heard about him murderin' that family."

"If I can extradite Shokely for those murders," the constable persisted, "his robbin' the stage will be secondary."

Brennen agreed with that, thanked Charley for the return of the money, assuring him he would send it along through to the claims division. Then both men parted.

Charley stopped before the window of the harness shop.

Jed beckoned. The coffee pot atop the small potbellied stove was giving off one of the most enticing aromas a man ever smelled.

Jed filled two cups, passed one to the constable, and took the second cup behind the counter. He said: "I saw you take that Smith *hombre* up to the corral yard in irons."

Charley nodded and remarked irrelevantly: "Texans don't care much for outlaws."

"How about the other one?"

"He'll go to Montana as soon as I get the papers to send him there."

"The story is goin' around about him killin' that woman an' little girl. You gotta add that to his havin' a hand in shootin' down the Terwilligers."

Charley sipped coffee before speaking again. "I can't prove nothin' on him when it comes to Frank and Judah P. Nothin' we saw up there contradicted what both of them strangers said. But where in hell did that get started about what happened in Montana?"

"Is it true?"

Charley set his half-emptied cup aside and said only: "Thanks."

He left the shop. The sun was fully up now, and, although it was bright enough, until the next spring it wouldn't really put out much warmth, not even if a man stood directly in its path.

Chapter Eleven

A PLEASANT EVENING,
AN UNPLEASANT MORNING

Lewis Boles brought in a dented tripod he'd found in Cache Cañon. Charley put it aside. He didn't ask if the instrument the tripod had supported had been found. Boles twisted a shapeless old hat in both hands as he reminded Charley that the riders were due to be paid in another few days. All Charley could tell him was that the heir up in Cheyenne had neither answered his letter nor arrived in Rock City. He offered one encouraging comment. "Give 'em another few days."

Boles asked: "An' after that? We been talkin'. We could cut out enough beef for our wages, drive 'em to a railhead, an' sell 'em."

Charley's reply was negative. "Without a bill of sale that'd be cattle stealin'. Give 'em another few days, a week or so."

"I hear you let one of those strangers go," Boles said in an accusatory tone.

"Didn't let him go, Lew. I sent him in chains down to Brownsville, Texas, where he's wanted for bank robbery."

"What about the other one?"

"He's still in his cell."

"You plannin' on sending him somewhere else, too?"

"I will if Montana wants to extradite him to be tried for three murders up there, maybe more."

"What about the murders he committed right here?"

"Murder is murder, Lew. You can only hang a man once."

"Yeah, mebbyso. He could also escape on the way up to Montana, or get let off by a judge."

"I don't expect he'll get off, Lew. There's a powerful lot of evidence against him. More for a fact than I have to prove he murdered George Crittenden."

"The hell with Crittenden! What about the Terwilligers?"

"I'll not argue that point with you, Lew. You were over the ground. You know pretty well what happened. You've seen the bodies. Bringin' in that tripod shows you been up there again. Frank and Judah P. were killed in a gunfight they probably started. They were armed. They were shooting. The strangers shot back."

"If the Terwilligers started the shootin', they was only protectin' their own land."

Charley shook his head in exasperation. "Believe me, Lew, this here Al Shokely will get tried and hanged in Montana. Now, let that be an end to it."

Boles was obviously furious, but he said no more. He simply walked out.

Once Boles had left, Charley went over to the Emporium to peek into the pigeon hole where his mail was deposited. It was empty. The buxom woman came to ask if Charley was expecting a letter. She said the southbound stage from Cheyenne had come in earlier that morning — something Charley had known for years — but that the mail hadn't been sorted as yet. It should be sorted by noon.

Charley looked around the store. The glass in the showcases shone, but George Crittenden's conveniently placed brass spittoons were gone and so was the mousy clerk. In his place was a woman young enough to be Charley's daughter. She returned Charley's casual appraisal with a steady, stony look.

The husky proprietoress said: "She's an old friend from back East. Anything else I can do for you, Constable?"

Outside, Charley's attention was caught by the arrival of the midday coach from the south. The horses were dry. He smiled. Sam Brennen had fired several whips who came into his corral yard with lathered animals.

Over at the jailhouse he encountered Jim Neely who barely let Charley get past the door before blurting out: "What about settling up for my three horses?"

Charley went to his desk, sat down, and considered the liveryman. "How much was they worth?" he asked.

He received a reply that did not surprise him. "Them was three of my best saddle animals, Constable. I've turned down offers to sell 'em."

Charley nodded. "What was they worth?"

"Well, figurin' they was in their prime an' as sound as new money, I'd say they was worth sixty dollars each."

"I can buy three sound horses with saddles for a lot less than that."

The liveryman fidgeted. "Fifty dollars, Constable?"

"Forty, includin' outfits."

Neely rolled his eyes heavenward and clutched his old hat. "The rigs wasn't much, but for a damned fact I could've peddled them horses for fifty dollars any time I was of a mind to."

"Forty dollars," Charley stated emphatically, and then added: "Maybe thirty . . . ?"

The liveryman replied quickly. "Forty dollars, Constable."

Charley fished in a trouser pocket, then counted out the money. "Write me a bill of sale. I'll come down an' pick it up later."

Neely departed, mumbling now under his breath.

After lunch at the café, Charley returned to the Emporium to check his box for mail. Neither of the women heeded his arrival, but the mail had been sorted, and at the postal desk he opened the first letter. It was from the same authorities to whom he had written in Montana. It was lengthy and had been signed by a fee lawyer. It said that, while the murder of a man named Burdett, his wife, and child was known and acknowledged, Montana had no dodger out for the murderer, except to offer a one-hundred-dollar reward for information leading to his arrest and conviction. The last sentence said that, if Constable Bent could provide proof that the man he was holding was the murderer, the Montana authorities would be pleased to see his proof before beginning any process of extradition.

Once back at the jailhouse, Charley brought Shokely into the office. When Charley said he'd heard from the Montana authorities, Shokely's reply was blunt.

"For what?"

Charley leaned forward with his hands on the desk. "It's up to you," he replied. "Sign a confession I'll write, or I'll ride out of town."

If Shokely thought it was a bluff he'd just heard, he steadily regarded Charley as he replied. "I know the law, Constable. You set me up for a lynchin', an' when word gets around you done it deliberately, you'll be in more trouble than you can shake a stick at."

Charley stood a moment longer, trading stares with Shokely, before he finally jerked his head back toward the cell block.

As the constable was locking Shokely in his strap-steel cage, the prisoner said: "Nobody's goin' to lynch me."

Charley returned to his office to think. There was the money Jed had brought in, having received it from the hold-outs. It was possible that he might make a charge of stage robbery stick, but he wasn't sure. He was in the act of crossing to the door when it was opened from the street side by a woman. She was probably in her fifties, but looked younger. She had hazel-colored eyes that matched her hair. On each side above the ears there were silver wings. There was a touch of brunette hair above her forehead. She smiled. "Constable Bent?"

Charley stepped back for the woman to enter. He pointed to a chair. She was dressed in rusty maroon. It highlighted her face. When she smiled, Charley self-consciously smiled back.

He went behind his desk, sat down, and waited. It was a short wait. She handed him an opened envelope, the same one he had mailed to Frank Terwilliger's heir up in Cheyenne. He held the envelope in both hands as she spoke again. "I'd say from your expression you didn't expect a woman."

It was the truth.

"My name is Amelia Thatcher."

Charley finally spoke. The only thing he could think of to say had to do with the wages shortly to be due the Terwilliger range men. Charley Bent hadn't lived as long as he had without seeing handsome women, but this one. . . . She scattered his thoughts.

"I'll see that they're paid. Is there someone in Rock City that I could hire to drive me to the ranch?"

There was the liveryman. There was also Sam Brennen who hired out rigs. Charley asked if she was staying at the hotel.

Her smile returned. "Not out of choice, Constable, but I did check in there when I arrived earlier today."

Charley could agree with her feeling. The Rock City hotel was a boar's nest. He had lived there for years because there was no other place. He told her he would do whatever he could for her. Once she had departed, he breathed deeply of the scent of lavender.

Charley had never been more than passingly interested in women. As a young man he'd seldom been where a range man met women. As an older man he'd known women — rancher's wives, dance-hall girls, an occasional widow — but to the best of his recollection none had ever left the scent of lavender or

123

had had such a beautiful smile. He decided to go up to the harness shop. Jed Ames was younger, but probably more experienced when it came to women.

Jed's shop was locked, and there was no sign of its proprietor. Charley then went to Finney's Pleasure Palace where Cork, the lifelong reader of faces and moods, set forth a bottle and a jolt glass without intruding on the constable's now very evident reverie.

The next morning Charley went down to the livery barn for his bill of sale and got a surprise. No one had hired a rig to drive out to the Terwilliger place. He got the bill of sale and went up to the corral yard where a hosteler also told him no one had hired a rig.

His last hike was back up to the hotel, and there he got another surprise. Ray Kemp had registered Amelia Thatcher the previous morning, but she had not stayed the night. She already had checked out the previous afternoon.

It was late for a long horseback ride, but he left town, riding in the direction of the Terwilliger place. The sun was slanting and the air was cool. The leaves were turning. Charley noticed none of these things. He loped when he could; otherwise he walked his animal. With luck, he could make it to the Terwilliger place and back before nightfall, but that depended on how much time he spent at the ranch.

When he had the rooftops of the buildings in sight, he stood up in his stirrups, but the distance was still too great. Here he curbed an urge to travel at a lope and came leisurely down the eastern slope with the yard well in sight. There was a buggy near the barn with both shafts on the ground. When he was close enough, he got a shock. That buggy had belonged to George Crittenden. It was identifiable from a fair distance by its red undercarriage and yellow wheels.

As he reached the tie rack in front of the barn and swung down to loop the reins and loosen the cinch, Lewis Boles emerged from the barn's double doors. If he was surprised to see the constable, he gave no indication of it. Boles motioned with his head in the direction of the ranch house. "If you're lookin' for Miz Thatcher, she's up there. She paid us. Me 'n' the boys was plannin' on goin' into town later."

"I'm glad things have worked out. Is the new owner plannin' on stayin'?"

"She is." Boles paused, anger coming to his eyes. "You heard from Montana yet?"

Charley didn't like to say it, but he did. "I'm afraid that Montana business didn't pan out the way I'd hoped."

"You still got that stranger in jail?"

"I do, but I'm not sure how long I can hold him. I hope to get him to confess to robbin' the stage."

Boles spat to the side, nodded to the constable, his sense of disgust obvious, and turned back toward the barn.

Charley crossed the yard, climbed the low, broad steps, and rattled the door with a ham-sized fist. When the door opened, he felt the same half-breathless sensation as when she had entered the jailhouse, and the smile was as handsome. He removed his hat to gain time. When he finally spoke, the words sounded lame even to him. "Couldn't find you in town, ma'am."

She moved aside for him to enter. The place didn't smell like it had when the Terwilligers had lived in it, but there was obviously little that could be done about the old, large, stone fireplace whose facing boulders were black from years of soot or the furnishings, which were scanty and scarred. The only light came from two small, front-wall windows.

Amelia Thatcher waited for Charley to speak.

He said: "You hired the Crittenden rig?"

Without replying at once, she invited him to be seated. Charley went docilely to the chair she had indicated, sat with his hat in both hands, between his knees.

She said: "I didn't hire it. I bought it from the storekeeper. The buggy and the big mare. She seemed very nice."

Charley had no comment to make about the big woman. "It's a right nice buggy, ma'am. George was proud of it. It's got a place in back for a fair-sized load."

She nodded, not quite smiling. "I understand George Crittenden, who owned it, also owned the Emporium. Did you know him well?"

"Yes, ma'am."

"His niece told me he was found shot in the office of the store."

Charley nodded, and then changed the subject. "I met Lew Boles outside. He says you're plannin' to stay on here."

"Yes. I asked him and the other hands to stay on with me. They were paid today, and I told them as they could go on into town later to celebrate. Don't you think that's a good idea . . . my staying on . . . for a while, anyway?"

Charley bobbed his head again.

Amelia Thatcher was more at ease with the constable than he was with her. She asked if Charley had any idea of the size of the Terwilliger holdings. When he answered that he had no idea, except that they were extensive, she responded: "Six thousand deeded acres."

In spite of himself, Charley looked shocked. Like others in the Cache Valley country he had assumed Frank and Judah P. had owned at least five times that much land. They had certainly given that impression.

She told Charley she had found the deeds in a dented tin box in Frank's office and had had to break the box open with a chisel. Her next question suggested to Charley that, despite

126

her handsome and warm smile, she was no average housewife, if, indeed, she had ever been one. "I don't know much about ranching, Mister Bent, but it seems to me my father and his brother were running about four times as many cattle as they had a legal right to run."

Charley had been in Cache Valley for years. It was, as was most stock country west of the Missouri River, open range. The first stockmen pretty well staked their claims. Subsequent settlers had respected them. There were thousands of acres of land to which the first comers had not only laid claim, and to the best parts, but had also backed up their claims to it with guns and torches. It had always taken Charley time to absorb shock. It did now, but he eventually asked if what she had in mind was cutting down the herds to fit the much smaller allotment of real land.

As before she smiled. "I've only been here a short while, Constable. Where I came from is also stock country, but I'm a widow. My husband was a land broker in Wyoming. I learned from him about legal rights and the claims of the first comers. There were some land and livestock wars up there. There still are. What I've learned since coming here is that the Terwilligers were hard men. They kept people off what they claimed was their land when, in fact, only a small portion of it was legally theirs. Mister Bent, can you tell me if it's possible to make a living from six thousand acres?"

Charley had to fumble with that question. He had been a range man in his youth, but a rider, nothing more. The economics of ranching were something he knew almost nothing about. His answer would be unsatisfactory, and he knew it as he gave it. "I got no idea whether you can make it on only six thousand acres. What I do know is that, if you cut back, you're goin' to lose a lot of possible income." Charley stopped moving his hat and looked straight at her. "No one's goin' to question the Terwilliger rights. The other stockmen have accepted them rights for years. I kind of doubt that it'd be a good idea to cut back."

As dusk arrived, she invited him to stay for supper. Charley accepted. Boles and the other hands had ridden out some time before. Their conversation continued through the meal, and when they adjourned back to the parlor.

Once Charley did leave, Amelia Thatcher stood on the porch and waved after him. He waved back, set his animal into an easy lope, and was so deeply in thought that he had Rock City's lights in his face before he realized how much ground he had covered.

The town was unusually quiet. Even Finney's Pleasure Palace, although lighted, sent forth into the darkened main street none of its customary noise. Charley saw that his horse was cared for without noticing the unusual reticence of the hosteler, and bypassed the jailhouse to walk the full distance to the hotel.

Ray Kemp was nowhere in sight. Charley climbed the stairs to his room, lighted the lamp, and took a long time kicking out of his boots, draping the shell belt and leathered Colt on its peg at the bedside, and spent some time at the only window. It faced southward, overlooking the full length of the main street in that direction.

There was a light at the harness shop, which was unusual. Jed Ames usually retired with the chickens, but Charley had known the harness maker sometimes to work later.

What had impressed him at the Terwilliger place was what the handsome woman had said, particularly her questions about cutting the Terwilliger herd back to what the deeded land would carry. As he had told her then, it was not unheard of in open range country for stockmen to take and hold as much land as they could. In a way, though, it was the fraudulent claim the Terwilligers had on Cache Cañon that had occasioned their deaths. He sighed as he turned away from the window.

Only a woman would even think of such a thing as giving up a land claim, and the implications were beyond his appreciation. He had been an open-range man since his youth. It had never really been a question of who actually owned the land. It had been traditionally who could claim the range and hold it. In the Cache Valley country, the Terwilligers had staked their claim early and had used whatever means were necessary to maintain their claim, including guns. Then he reflected how the widow woman from Cheyenne was also a mighty fine cook.

Once in bed, Charley slept well. When he awakened, he took his towel, soap, and razor out back to the wash house. When, upon his return, Charley had passed the kitchen and caught the scent of frying meat, there was still no sign of Ray Kemp.

Out front of the hotel, with the chilly morning somehow not quite free of the night's long shadows even though the sun was up, Charley was again struck with the feeling of quiet foreboding. The main street was empty. It might be so because, after all, it was breakfast time. Charley stretched, heard a muted curse from the corral yard, and twisted.

At the north end of Rock City was an ancient, gnarled oak. It had several perpendicular limbs that reached almost to the ground. Several of those limbs had old rope burns. It was known locally as the hanging tree.

Charley froze. A battered corpse hung in motionless suspension from one of the lower limbs.

For ten seconds Charley stood rooted before he walked as close as was necessary. He suspected who the dead man might be, and, upon closer inspection, found he was right. The murderer of a little girl, her mother, and father was as limp as a rag. His color was putty gray.

Charley stood a moment, then turned, and hiked as far south as the jailhouse. The heavy door he had locked from the outside before leaving town the previous day had been savagely attacked until the big, old brass lock had been shattered. The door yielded to the slightest push. Inside, where Charley's keys were kept on a peg, there were no keys. He went back to the cell block, and here at least there were abundant signs of a struggle. Here, too, he found the keys on the floor near the open cell door.

He had awakened hungry. Now, as he returned to his office where there were fewer signs of disturbance, he sank down at the desk with no appetite.

Chapter Twelve

AFTERMATH

Everything Charley had done after emerging from the hotel had been seen by dozens of watching eyes, but no one approached the jailhouse until he was reaching for his hat, then Jed Ames walked in.

"It wasn't no secret, Charley," Jed confessed to the constable. "Ray Kemp told Cork at the saloon about them pieces of paper."

Jed sat down. He hadn't removed his apron. He waited, and, when Charley did not speak, he continued. "Not everyone was in favor of hangin' the son-of-a-bitch, but mostly they were. An' you was out of town."

Charley broke his silence. "Who were the ring leaders?"

Jed shook his head. "There wasn't none. It was a mob."

"Mostly from the saloon?" Charley asked dryly.

Jed shook his head again. "Some from the saloon, some from other places. If you mean everyone was carryin' half a load from Cork's place, you're wrong. Charley, what that man done in Montana couldn't have no excuse anywhere I ever been, and then there was the death of George Crittenden, and what happened to the Terwilligers. It all adds up to a lot ag'in' one man."

Charley eyed his friend.

Jed read his thoughts. "I leaned on the rope. So did others . . . Charley."

"It's done," the constable said. "Can't be undone."

The harness maker nodded. "He's been cut down and

131

hauled to the carpenter's shop. Doc Reese wasn't involved, but he also don't seem to be sheddin' any tears."

Charley let go a ragged sigh. In all his years as a lawman he'd never before had a prisoner taken from him, and, if he'd been in town, it wouldn't have happened this time. On the other hand, the cool way the authorities up in Montana had replied to his letter — well, Shokely did have it coming by whatever means. What rankled was that the lynchers had waited until he was out of town. He looked sharply at Jed Ames, who rose nervously to depart.

"I s'pose the Terwilliger range men were involved?"

The harness maker nodded.

"Jed, if this ever happens again while I'm constable. . . ."

"It most likely won't, Charley. It likely wouldn't have happened this time, except that there's a lot of folks in town who've got wives an' little girls, an' some cottoned to George Crittenden . . . and even the Terwilligers. If we hadn't done it, what would have happened?"

"Nothin', pro'bly. I'd've had to let him go." Charley sighed again. "Well, plant the son-of-a-bitch. . . ."

Jed promised to see that it was done.

Charley went to breakfast. The slovenly caféman avoided looking at him. Nor did he say a word when he served the constable, after which he went back to his kitchen without returning until Charley was gone.

There was an interlude shortly after midday when Amelia Thatcher arrived in town, with Lewis Boles driving the Crittenden rig. She had the rig parked in front of the general store and crossed to the jailhouse. When she entered, she was not smiling. Charley guessed what was coming and prepared himself for it. He motioned her to a chair.

The handsome woman said: "I've brought Lew Boles to town with me. He told me early on about the fight in Cache

132

Cañon. And now I also know about what happened last night."

Charley met her gaze without flinching. "There wasn't much I could do about it. You know where I was when it happened. Did Lew tell you that there was no way to prove murder against any of those strangers for the deaths of your father and your uncle? I don't doubt Al Shokely killed George Crittenden, but without a confession I couldn't really have proved it in court before the circuit judge. Montana didn't have enough proof, either, to charge him with the deaths of that family up there, but that's where Shokely got the map to where the cache was hidden. He admitted that much. An' that's why they were in Cache Cañon to begin with. It could be they opened up on Frank and Judah P., an' not the other way around. Smith, who's been extradited to Texas, wouldn't say so. Leathergood is dead, killed in the gun battle. That left Shokely, an' he wasn't talkin'."

"Mister Boles said it looked to him like it had been a fair fight, but he wasn't sure, and that didn't excuse the strangers for being on Terwilliger land. Only, as I was saying yesterday, Cache Cañon certainly isn't deeded land. It would appear the strangers had as much right there as my father or uncle."

Charley leaned back onto the desk. "For the sake of us bein' friends, Miz Amelia, I'll say I'm sorry . . . all the way around."

Her response shocked Charley. "I didn't know my father, but I did know my mother. She never said much against him but, Mister Bent, a man who would desert her the way he did couldn't make another woman like him. Mother had to work very hard to keep us both alive. Frank sent her money from time to time, but it was never very much. Now that I've seen his papers, I know he could have done much better by us. I'm sorry he was killed, but in my moments of thinking how wonderful it would be to have a father like other girls did . . . well, he wasn't that far away. From Rock City to Cheyenne is no more than a two-day ride."

Charley had some private thoughts. From what he knew of Frank Terwilliger, he would not have made a good father, particularly to a daughter. A son might have fared better, but that was also somewhat questionable.

"I never knew my father, Constable. But what I've seen and heard since coming here doesn't make me especially sad about never knowing him."

"I really can't speak to that, ma'am. But in view of what just happened in this here town, I'm not goin' to comment on making any quick final judgments."

"I'm not judging my father, Mister Bent. His death was senseless, but somehow it was also consistent with the way he lived his life." Amelia Thatcher then fixed Charley with a very steady gaze. "That talk about a cache . . . ?"

"Just that, ma'am . . . talk . . . as far as I know. Whoever named that cañon up yonder and the countryside likely had reasons, but I've been in a dozen places where stories like that are common, an' I can tell you for a fact there's potholes by the score where folks've dug, an' no one's ever found anything." Charley smiled a little. "I reckon it's a fairy tale."

She cocked her head a little. "Is it also a fairy tale that there are renegade Indians north of Cache Cañon?"

The way she said it, and the way she was looking at him, convinced Charley that she had heard about the Indians, possibly from those who had seen them. His answer was carefully given.

"Ma'am, there was soldiers here a few days back. They left town satisfied there wasn't any Injuns up yonder."

She almost smiled at him. "May I ask you a direct question?"

"Yes'm."

"Did you see Indians up there?"

Charley cleared his throat, got up from sitting on the desk, but seemed reluctant to answer.

Amelia Thatcher laughed as she rose from the chair. At the door she asked: "Would you do me a favor?"

Charley nodded.

"Come to the ranch again, when you can."

He nodded again, and she closed the door after herself.

"Damned Injuns," Charley said to himself.

Then he went into the cell block and began cleaning up the cell where Shokely had been imprisoned. Next he went to work on the outer office until there was scarcely any sign of what had happened the previous night. The last thing he did before crossing the road to the café was to drape the cell-room keys on their peg near the gun rack.

As he had his midday meal, he thought of something. By all rights Amelia Thatcher should have Frank's will. He would take it out to her.

By mid-afternoon the constable was feeling better. He had gone to see Sam Brennen at the corral-yard office. Brennen hadn't admitted to being a party to the lynching, but he did say that the presence of the amount of money that had been stolen on the strangers and the confession Charley had obtained concerning their involvement did certainly justify what had happened, particularly when added to Shokely's other crimes.

Following the meeting with Brennen, Charley visited the saloon where Cork Finney had some difficulty in meeting the constable's direct gaze. After a jolt, Charley said: "I could start me a list of them lynchers just from the looks on their faces when we meet."

The saloonman was blunt, more so than Jed Ames. "It wasn't no conspiracy, Charley. We didn't deliberately wait until

135

you was out of town. It just happened that way. And do you know what that son-of-a-bitch said before he was hanged? He said that you'd told him you were going to leave town just so the rest of us *could* hang him. Did you say that to Shokely, Charley?"

"Well . . . yes, I said it, but it was only a bluff to make him talk."

Cork leaned against his side of the bar. "An' you did ride out, Charley. So don't say you didn't have no hand in what happened."

Charley reddened and would have fired back an answer, but Andy Buck walked in, accompanied by one-legged Lex Morton. All three exchanged nods. Lex Morton offered to stand a round.

Andy Buck said: "That there lady who bought George's buggy . . . well, Lex seen her 'n' them women at the store, actin' real cozy."

Charley regarded Lex, who had downed his jolt and was in the act of pushing the little glass toward Cork for a refill. "What does cozy mean?"

Lex downed his second jolt before answering. "Well, it was sort of like they was sisters, sort of pattin' each other." The former soldier had clearly seen more of the world than the men around him. "It ain't often, but sometimes women cotton to one another."

"Friends?" Cork asked.

"More'n that," Lex replied, looking sly. "When I was young, there was a couple like that where I come from, a place called Magnolia Springs in Alabama. It scandalized the hell out of folks."

Jed Ames now walked in without his apron. He nodded to the others and jerked his head for the constable to follow him outside. Shadows were gathering, but neither man heeded that.

136

Jed said: "You still got that map of Cache Cañon?"

Charley nodded.

"Well, a long, lanky feller arrived this afternoon and was askin' around about how to find the cañon."

Charley almost sighed. "Is he still in town?"

The harness maker didn't know.

Charley went down to the livery barn where Jim Neely told him a lanky stranger had given him a silver dollar for feed for his horse and had talked about getting out to the Cache Cañon area.

Charley considered the lowering sun. By the time he could reach Cache Cañon, it would be dark. He would make the ride in the morning instead, but the prospect wasn't pleasant.

Before he retired for the night, he wondered if he really had to make that ride, anyway. What decided him that he must do it was the possibility that an exploring stranger might ride up the trail out of Cache Cañon. Chances were the hold-outs wouldn't bother him. After all, they had been eluding detection for years. But the possibility also existed that, if the stranger rode up there, he might do something foolish and get himself shot the way Leathergood had, not by the Terwilligers but this time by the Indians. He finally went to bed feeling more disgusted than sleepy. That damned cache was going to attract people as long as there was talk of its existence.

Charley rose early and grained his horse before going to the café where he was the first customer of the day. He was bundled against the morning chill and did not look happy when the caféman asked if he planned on being gone long. Charley eyed the slovenly man over the rim of his coffee cup as he answered.

"What difference would it make? There's no one left to lynch."

The caféman slunk back to his cooking area and did not return until Charley rose to depart, and then he glared in the direction of the door, but said nothing. The caféman hadn't actually leaned on the hang rope, but he had used his bulk to help overcome Shokely in his cell.

There had never been a way for a rider, crossing open grassland, not to be seen, but this time Charley did not care. He rode with doubts, not only about some long-shanked stranger seeking Cache Cañon, but of what his purpose might be in riding toward the uplands at all.

When he was nearing the mouth of the cañon, he heard a horse nicker. When he advanced past the trees and could see the area around the old, log house, he saw the man. He seemed as tall as Abe Lincoln was said to have been. The man had his back to Charley. He was busy using a spyglass, and, when he turned, Charley was squarely in his sight. He lowered the glass, pushed it into itself, also hastily pocketed a small book he'd been writing in, and called a greeting from in front of the old house.

Charley returned the greeting by waving as he dismounted and led his horse the rest of the way. After loosening his riding coat, he introduced himself, but he did not smile or offer a hand. The other man was half a head taller and lean. He had a beard shadow. He also had a beak for a nose, thin lips, and a nervous manner when he spoke.

"I didn't expect company," he told Charley, "but you're welcome. Too late for breakfast, I'm afraid."

So far the stranger had not done or said anything to soften the constable's mood of irritability. He asked a pointblank question. "You got a reason for bein' up here, mister?"

"Well, yes," the tall man replied. "But not exactly here by this old shack. I came in here last night to bed down out of the cold."

Charley repeated the question. "You got a reason for bein' up here?"

"My name's Edward Southerland. I do surveyin' and platting for the railroad people." Southerland gestured southward with a skinny long arm. "Beyond this cañon . . . maybe about a couple hundred yards . . . my job is to line out the best route for the laying of track."

Charley relaxed. "The best route, mister, would be for the railroad to use the north-south road which is about two, three miles east from here."

Southerland smiled. "I've already platted for that, Constable. Took me three days. But the railroad folks don't want to run north and south. They like to avoid towns when they can. I'm figuring the track to go west to east. It'll be about eight miles or so north of Rock City."

Charley thought briefly of George Crittenden. If George could have heard this spindle-shanked stranger, he would have had a heart attack. He loosened slightly toward the surveyor. "When does the railroad figure to start laying track?"

"Oh, it'll be at least a year, maybe two. Once I turn in my findings, they have to be approved by the company's directors, subjected to approval by stockholders, and even the federal government and the financiers who'll put up the capital. Maybe longer than two years."

Charley gazed in the direction of the high bluff, saw nothing up there, and turned to snug up his cinch. Then, again in the saddle, he said: "I'm not sure, Mister Southerland, but that country you described might belong to the Terwilliger ranch."

Southerland was not the least alarmed. "That's part of the process," he said simply. "Some of the preliminary work, after the surveying, is for land agents to visit land owners and offer to buy a right of way."

Charley returned the way he had come. He was tempted to

visit the Terwilliger place. He had a fair excuse, after talking with the railroad surveyor, but he had forgotten to take along Frank's will. He rode directly back to Rock City. There was no denying he was attracted to Amelia Thatcher, but several things bothered him, not the least was what Lex Morton had said at the saloon. Although he was not clear in his mind what had been meant, he had heard whispers about such things, and he was actually not clear in his mind about all the implications.

Back in town he encountered Sam Brennen, who for once was not waspish, but he was one of those high-strung individuals who always shot from the hip. They met in front of the harness shop. Sam had an armload of patched halters. He asked if Charley had heard there was another stranger in town who had been asking directions to Cache Cañon.

Charley nodded without explaining that he'd trailed the stranger and had talked to him.

Sam began: "If he's another highwayman. . . ."

Charley thinly smiled. "He ain't."

"You're sure?"

"Can't often be sure about anythin', Sam, but I'll keep an eye on him."

Brennen cast a quick look at the constable. "You do that," he said, and hiked in the direction of the corral yard.

Jed Ames appeared in the shop doorway, wiping both hands on an oily cloth. "That lady who's got the Terwilliger place was lookin' for you." Jed jutted his jaw. "That's George's buggy out front of the Emporium."

Charley thanked Jed for the information and went down to the store where the buxom woman and her somewhat diminutive clerk were clearly trying to delay the handsome woman's departure. When Charley appeared, the new proprietor glared, and the face of the clerk reddened. Amelia Thatcher greeted Charley like an old friend and crossed to the jailhouse with

140

him, leaving the other two women looking venomously at the constable.

When they were inside, Amelia Thatcher said: "I don't know why but they make me uncomfortable."

Charley did not comment. He fumbled in a drawer and withdrew Frank's will, which he held out. She accepted it, and, as Charley spoke, she put it in a pocket.

He told her about the railroad surveyor in Cache Cañon. He also told her why the man was up there. She frowned. "A railroad?"

"It's been talked about for some time, ma'am. In fact, the feller who used to own the Emporium was very much in favor of it." Charley smiled a little. "He'll never know that they plan to skirt the foothills with their tracks an' not come south to Rock City, which he figured would make the town grow."

Amelia seemed only passingly interested in all this. She asked if Charley had heard that local stockmen had been missing a beef now and then, and that this was being attributed to the hold-out Indians in the mountains.

Charley had been hearing this for years, and, while he'd never taken it seriously, since his meeting atop the bluff with Running Horse and Man Who Hunts, he was willing to accept it as the truth. He evaded a direct answer by saying: "When stock range over thousands of acres, ma'am, it ain't unusual for 'em to miss a beef now an' then when they gather."

She seemed to accept this explanation and mentioned something else. If it would be possible for him to ride to her ranch, she'd like him to go buggy-riding with her to help find some steel pipes driven into the ground by her father to mark Terwilliger deeded land.

Charley agreed to ride out the following morning, although he told her he had no idea where those boundary markers might be. As she left, she smiled. "Mister Boles told me where he'd seen two of those pipes."

Once she was gone, Charley wondered why she didn't have Lewis Boles help her find those markers, but he did not wonder long. She had asked him to go with her, and, whatever that presaged, Charley Bent was perfectly agreeable.

Chapter Thirteen

TWO PEOPLE AND AUTUMN

People noticed Charley's departure from town with little interest. For one thing, the constable had been riding out quite a bit lately. For another thing, the morning he left Rock City was one of the first days of full-fledged autumn with all that implied, from men donning their long johns for winter to women folk starting the arduous task of putting up for winter.

Charley had been wearing the same pelt-side-in riding coat for years. He was comfortable inside it even when bitter cold arrived. His gloves were also lined with sheep pelt. His animal's breath came like steam. As far as a man could see, it was clear as glass. The few mammy cows he saw had their winter hair and their calves, having been dropped no later than March, were big, sassy, and no longer interested in their mothers, which was just as well because, as the graze had gone to seed, their milk had dried up.

When he had the Terwilliger yard in sight, someone was already rigging out a stud-necked mare while another man was leaning on the tie rack, smoking. It was this second man who saw Charley and said something that brought the first man briefly around. When he returned to his work, he seemed to move a little faster.

When Charley reached the yard, the loafing man raised an arm. Charley did the same, approached the tie rack, and dismounted. The second man held out his hand for the reins. As he did this, he jerked his head. "She's at the house, Constable." The rider's face was expressionless, but, as Charley struck out for the ranch house, the man holding Charley's horse said something in a half whisper, and both men snickered.

When Amelia Thatcher opened the door, the sound and scent of a lighted fire provided a pleasant background. She was dressed for chilly weather and closed the door after Charley entered. The parlor was cheerful. Amelia had Charley take a chair and brought him a cup of hot coffee. When she sat, she said: "I wasn't sure you'd make it this morning but wanted to be prepared in case you did."

Charley had to unbutton his coat. Between the hot coffee and the blazing fire he felt warm. Amelia Thatcher brought forth a paper and handed it to the constable. He looked at it and reddened. He'd thought he'd given her Frank Terwilliger's will in the jailhouse yesterday. What he was holding in his hand was the map responsible for the deaths of several people including one small child. He told her of his mistake. "When next you're in town, I'll give you the will." He pocketed the map.

They had a second cup of coffee, and Charley had to shed his coat. Amelia Thatcher seemed in no hurry to leave the warm room for the autumn cold. She said: "Mister Boles told me about where he'd seen the pair of boundary pipes. He also told me he'd worked for the Terwilligers for six years. When I asked him about them, he said they weren't easy to work for until a man got to know them. He said Judah P. was unpredictable. Did you find him that way, Mister Bent?"

Charley held back. "They was different in most ways. Frank could be reasoned with. Judah P . . . well, he was different."

She smiled. "When we get back, would you like to stay for supper?"

Charley also smiled. "I'd like that. For a fact, you're a fine cook."

Her response was revealing. "My mother took in boarders.

144

She was a good cook. She taught me from the time I was about seven or eight." Her expression softened. "She rarely smiled or laughed, but she was a wonderful person."

Charley held his empty coffee cup in both hands and gently turned it. If Amelia Thatcher's mother had been a wonderful person, regardless of her problems, whether she knew it or not, or whether the opportunity had been offered to her or not, the best thing fate had done for her was see she didn't have the opportunity to marry Frank Terwilliger and so come to live in this same house with that bleak man and his unpredictable brother.

Amelia Thatcher put her cup aside, stood up, and reached for her coat. Charley took his cue from this and got back into his rider's coat.

The change from the warm house to the yard was sharply noticeable. The big buggy mare was dozing. There was no sign of the range hands. Charley untied the mare. The woman got into the rig and unlooped the lines.

As they drove out of the yard, a rider appeared in the bunkhouse doorway briefly, then turned to speak over his shoulder. "Poke another piece of wood in the stove. Is it my deal?" He closed the door.

Charley hadn't ridden in a buggy in a long time and was very conscious of the woman who seemed always to smell faintly of lavender. She drove as though she had a destination, which she did have. When they had gone westerly several miles, she said: "It should be close to a large oak."

Charley raised his arm. There were some spindly oaks but only one gnarled, old one. The woman drove toward it.

They had to stamp down dead weeds before Charley found the stake and stood beside it, considering the lay of the land. He told Amelia Thatcher that, from what little he knew of property lines, the direction from this stake could be north, south, or west. She agreed, got back into the rig, and drove in an angling, northeasterly direction. She told Charley the second iron pipe was in that direction according to Lewis Boles.

A cold breeze came off the highlands. Amelia Thatcher, who had been raised in this kind of country, ignored it. So did Charley, but for a different reason. Every time they ground over a hummock of buffalo grass or had two wheels sink into a depression, they touched at the hip and shoulder. Charley was surprised at himself. He could see far enough ahead to brace against this touching, but he did not do it.

When they had the mouth of Cache Cañon in sight, he did not say it, but he did not believe they were heading in the right direction. Yet, she had the lines and was clearly following a course given by the range boss. As they reached the mouth of the cañon, she drew rein. Charley finally suggested that they might be too far north. The reply he got was given in a firm voice. "It's around here somewhere. It has to be."

They dropped tether weight and walked. Here, at the entrance to Cache Cañon, there was trampled undergrowth that made the search easier, but after about an hour of seeking the iron pipe in several directions Charley asked the woman how long ago Lew had found the marker. When she said he'd told her it had been several years earlier, Charley wondered aloud if they'd find it because it was the nature of grazing cattle to scratch on anything they encountered. She may have considered this, but the constable learned one thing about Amelia Thatcher: she had a stubborn streak.

They drove in a large circle and did not find the pipe until Charley saw a wisp of something bright yellow back near the entrance to Cache Cañon. Why they hadn't seen it earlier was because of a flourishing thornpin bush. Until the brisk little ground swell of a breeze made the yellow marker flutter in the topmost branches of the bush, it had not been noticeable. They

146

drove back. Charley climbed out, used his heavy gloves to push branches aside, and called to Amelia Thatcher. "Whoever drove this into the ground must have done it years back. This bush is dang near as tall as I am."

She leaned to see the pipe and straightened up slowly. "How did that piece of yellow ribbon get there?" she asked.

Charley had already arrived at an explanation. "That surveyor I met up in the cañon likely put it there to show where the boundary marker is."

Charley paused to study the land. The fight in the cañon when the Terwilligers had encountered the strangers had been caused because Frank and Judah P. were convinced they had been trespassing on Terwilliger land. If that iron pipe was in the right place, it marked where Terwilliger land ran east and west and did not include the cañon.

Charley did not mention this on the drive back to the yard. He had a reason. If the railroad was going to run east and went several hundred yards south of the cañon, which would be well south of the iron pipe, then the tracks would cross Terwilliger deeded land. Neither of them said much on the drive back. While the little breeze had blown itself out, the cold had increased. By the time they reached the yard, they could both feel it. Charley said the forthcoming night was going to be bitterly cold.

Lewis Boles had seen them coming and was waiting at the tie rack. He asked if they'd located the pipes and seemed pleased that they had, as he led the mare into the barn to be unharnessed, stalled, and fed.

At the main house there were coals but no fire. Charley went out back for an armload of wood, coaxed the fire to burn, and stood with his back to it. Amelia Thatcher came to stand beside him. She said she'd make supper, and Charley shed his heavy coat for the second time. He remained standing by the

147

fireplace after Amelia Thatcher disappeared into the kitchen. He was still standing like that when she called him to join her.

How she managed to make the kind of meal she put on the table, using the battered cooking equipment the Terwilligers had left behind, was a mystery, but the supper was a triumph in Charley's eyes, who had been eating in disreputable cafés most of his life.

He helped with the dishes and, afterwards, took her to the parlor, asked for a piece of paper and a pencil, which she found for him, and with daylight fast fading outside knelt on the floor near the fireplace and used its light to draw several lines. When he was finished, he explained.

"This here is where we found the first marker." She was kneeling beside him when she nodded. "Follow that line to where we found the second pipe."

She said: "It's a straight line. Northeastward."

He sat back on his heels for a moment before drawing another line. "This is where that railroad surveyor said they'd lay tracks."

She looked up, frowning. "That's my land."

He smiled. "You was wonderin' about cuttin' back the cattle to run on your deeded land. You could do that, if you're of a mind. But my guess is that, when they got to buy a right of way across your north range, you could buy more land an' not have to sell down your critters."

She arose slowly, went to a battered cupboard, brought forth a dusty bottle, filled two small glasses, and handed one to Charley who had also risen. She said: "Would you mind terribly if I called you Charley?"

He held up his glass to brush the glass she was holding as he said: "If you didn't mind me callin' you Amelia."

They downed the whiskey. She was not entirely successful in repressing a shudder that Charley made a point of not noticing as he leaned to put his glass aside. She sank down in an old leather chair. He remained close to the fire, watching her.

When she finally faced him, she said: "You should have been a businessman, Charley."

His reply was tentative. "In my own way, Amelia, I am a businessman an', if I don't start back soon. . . ."

She got to her feet as he struggled into his coat. Her eyes were bright. Her face was slightly flushed, and not entirely from the whiskey. She seemed to want to say something, but he was heading for the door, hat in hand. He turned. "Amelia . . . ?"

"Charley?"

"It was a right fine supper, an' the buggy ride was real nice, too."

After he closed the door, she remained standing for several moments before approaching the fireplace to pick up the paper he'd drawn on and take it to a chair with her.

For Charley, upon whom the whiskey had little effect except to heighten his sense of warm well-being, the ride to town was long but pleasant. By the time he rode into the livery barn to hand his reins to the hosteler, he was satisfied with himself, but there was something he had to do before bedding down.

Sam Brennen was in his cramped and littered office. He was wearing a green eyeshade that he removed when the constable entered. There was a small, potbellied stove in a corner that popped and crackled.

Charley did not take a chair or loosen his coat. What he had come for wouldn't take long. He asked if that lanky stranger had left town and Brennen, who misunderstood Charley's interest, said: "Not that I know of. He sure didn't leave on a stage. Why? You figure he's another highwayman?"

Charley didn't answer as he left the office.

Up at the hotel there was a lighted, hanging lamp in the threadbare parlor but no sign of the hotelman. Charley went to Ray Kemp's door and knocked with a big fist. He had to do this three times before Kemp answered irritably.

"What do you want? I'm in bed."

Charley struck the door one more time. "Open up," he growled.

Kemp came to open the door attired in a long nightshirt and a tasseled night cap. He glared. "What'n hell won't keep until mornin', for Christ's sake?"

"You got a tall, skinny city man, Ray?"

Kemp sighed. "In room four. What'd he do?"

"Go back to bed," the constable said, and turned in the direction of the room with the number 4 painted in black on the middle of the door.

The hotelman leaned to watch. When the only recent paying guest Kemp'd had in several days opened the door, Constable Bent pushed inside and closed the door. Kemp went back to bed.

Edward Southerland was a tidy individual. He had two satchels placed side by side, and his matching breeches and coat were draped from a wooden hanger beneath which were his boots. Like Ray Kemp, Southerland slept in a long night dress with slits on each side, but, unlike Kemp, he wore no night cap. He had been asleep, and the arrival of the lawman who looked even larger in his riding coat was intimidating. Southerland pointed to the only chair in the room and retreated to his bed to perch on the edge of it.

Charley wasted no time. "I was up north today an' found a yellow rag in a bush."

Southerland's face cleared. "I found an iron marker in a bush. I put the yellow tag on it, so's I could see it from up a ways. Do you know what those iron pipes mean?"

150

"Years back the Terwilligers had a surveyor stake out their northern property line."

Southerland relaxed. "I figured it had to be something like that. Accordin' to my metes an' bounds, that stake was dead in place with another stake, but the second one wasn't in a bush. I could sight on it without a marker."

Charley had his answer, but he had more questions. "You're finished here?" he asked. When Southerland inclined his head, he continued: "I'd like to have the address of the railroad company, if you got it."

Southerland had it. He tore the top off his letter of authorization for making the survey and handed it to Charley, who read it and shoved the paper into a pocket. "By any chance do you do private surveyin'?"

Southerland smiled a little. "That's my business."

"If a man wanted to hire you, where would he write to?"

Southerland went to his hanging coat, brought forth a small, leather folder, extracted a card, and handed it to the constable. "Dollar a day, Mister Bent. Write me any time."

As Charley pocketed the card, he asked if Southerland would be leaving the vicinity soon.

Again the tall man nodded. "I intend to ride out in the morning."

Charley returned to his own room, shucked out of his boots, shell belt, hat, and outer clothing, and climbed into a bed as cold as a witch's teat. He didn't mind. In wintertime he'd rarely climbed into any other kind of bed.

He slept well, awoke hungry as a wolf, and went to the café. Cork Finney and Andy Buck were already at the counter. There were also several range men to whom Charley nodded.

The caféman came for Charley's order and got a surprise. The constable smiled at him as he ordered breakfast. In his cooking area the caféman thought it was nice that the local

151

lawman didn't appear to hold a grudge over the lynching. He had known Charley Bent too long to believe that by now the constable didn't have an idea who had been with the lynch mob.

Cork Finney said quietly. "There's talk."

Charley thanked the caféman for placing a mug of hot black java in front of him after which he looked at Cork. "There's always talk. What is it this time? Someone find that damned cache?"

"It's about you," Finney replied in the same low voice. "It's being said around town you're sweet on the woman who inherited the Terwilliger place."

Charley reddened, something the saloonman noticed as he went back to his meal. When the constable offered no rebuttal, Cork drained his coffee cup, arose, slid several coins beside his empty platter, slapped Charley lightly on the shoulder, and departed. He whistled all the way up to the saloon where he unlocked the door and got a fire going in the cannon heater. He tied on his apron and lighted his first cigar of the day, satisfied he had evidence of confirmation to the speculative gossip.

As for Charley, he went from the café to the jailhouse, dropped his hat atop the desk, sat down, and mingled his thoughts. One was what the railroad surveyor had told him, and the other was about Amelia Thatcher. The second thought held his interest longest.

Chapter Fourteen

AN AMIABLE STRANGER

The cold increased, but the sky remained clear. There would be no early snowfall. Jed Ames, Lex Morton, and Andy Buck went north in a wagon they hired from Jim Neely to get a start laying in firewood. It was late for doing this, so they bypassed a number of easily available, green trees and halted when they came across their first, dead cedar.

They would only take downed, dead, dry trees. Andy Buck and Jed manned the crosscut. Lex Morton stood by to trickle coal oil on the blade from time to time. The old man could split dry wood, but only if he kept his wooden leg exactly in place. Otherwise he would fall. He'd split his share of stove wood for many years and was an expert. They worked until noon, then rested, ate whatever they'd brought along, and afterwards worked again. They had about two-thirds of a load when a rider came through the trees where they were working.

He wasn't a tall man, and he had the weathered look of a competent range man. When he dismounted, he was as friendly as a setter pup. He said his name was Liam Baxter and he was from southern Wyoming where the snow already lay six inches deep.

If there was anything particularly noticeable about the man from Wyoming, it was that he wore his holstered Colt thonged to his leg, something neither town men nor range men did. He asked how close he was to Rock City, and they told him maybe a tad more than six miles. He said he had a friend there. He helped down another dead tree and split the rounds until they had about all Jed thought they should load. It was a light, dray wagon with steel springs, and they were sprung almost straight.

Liam Baxter rode a short-backed horse, muscled up where most horses didn't even have the place for muscles. His saddle had been made in Miles City, Montana, and had seen lots of use. He didn't slouch in the saddle, nor was he straight-backed, either. He had either been in Mexico or had done some trading with someone who had, since he wore a pair of deeply blued spurs with a lot of intricate silver inlay. Most range men owned spurs with some silver overlay, but the hooks Liam Baxter wore could almost be classified as jewelry. To buy a pair like that, made north of the border, would cost six month's wages.

Baxter was curious about Cache Valley, Rock City, and the outlying cow outfits. Jed ventured the opinion that, if he were looking for work, most of the local stockmen hired in springtime and laid off in autumn. Liam Baxter nodded about this, something he would certainly know as a seasonal rider, but offered no other reason he might be interested in the Cache Valley country. By the time the wood cutters reached town, Baxter left them to go his own way. Only Andy Buck made a vocal judgment while watching Baxter ride off. He said: "You get the feelin' that'd be a bad man to cross?"

If either Lex Morton or Jed Ames shared that feeling, neither of them said so.

They backed the wagon up beside Lex Morton's shack first and dumped a third of the wood. Their next stop was in the alley behind the harness shop where Jed and the blacksmith tossed down half of what remained, and their last stop was at the smithy, across the road from the livery barn. When the last of the wood had been dumped, Jed drove the old wagon around behind the livery barn.

As he removed the team from between the shafts, he heard

154

a familiar laugh. Liam Baxter and Jim Neely were part way up the runway, talking. As Jed listened, he made his own assessment of the stranger. Liam Baxter had one of those personalities that could charm a bird down out of a tree, but the questions he asked in his good-natured way struck the harness maker as more than just casual. The liveryman was explaining to Baxter how to reach the Terwilliger place. While Neely was doing this, he interrupted himself to say: "But the Terwilliger boys is dead, an' a woman that's Frank's bastard, which folks hereabout didn't know of, showed up to claim the outfit."

Baxter said: "That's interestin' ain't it?"

The liveryman agreed. "More'n just interestin', friend. Us folks that knew Frank would figure he'd be about the last person on earth to get tangled up with a woman."

Baxter and Neely laughed together. While he was still laughing, Baxter asked another question. "If she's a bastard, what name does she go by?"

"Thatcher. Amelia Thatcher."

The man from Wyoming handed the liveryman a silver dollar, admonished him that the horse's owner wanted only the best care for his animal, and left the barn.

Jed finished with the team, threw the harness in the bed of the wagon, and led the horses inside to be stalled and fed. The liveryman came along, looking pleasant. "Real nice feller left that good-lookin' horse. He's from Wyoming. Give me a cartwheel to look after his animal." Neely grinned from ear to ear. "For that kind of money I'd let the horse sleep with me."

Jed did not smile. He counted out silver for the use of the wagon and went up to the jailhouse. Charley was not there. So he went up to his shop, tied on the mulehide apron, and went to work.

The more he thought about the man from Wyoming, his geniality, his generosity with the liveryman, and the questions he'd asked, the more Jed worried. It wasn't Liam Baxter himself. No one could fault his helpfulness, his easy amiability. It was some of the things he had said culminating in the way he had pumped the liveryman while being the soul of friendliness. There was something else. Most men who rode horses and carried sidearms used a thong over their holstered weapons that crossed over where the hammer was and tied down on the far side. Liam Baxter's tie-down thong was through the trigger guard. Maybe that's the way they did it in Wyoming, but the inescapable fact was that it would take seconds less to yank the gun free than if the tie-down went over the holstered gun. It didn't have to mean much. In fact, none of the harness maker's uncharitable thoughts had to mean much. He'd misjudged men before.

As dusk arrived, he went over to the café. While the usual diners were at the counter, there was no sign of the constable. That didn't have to mean much, either. Lately Charley had been doing a lot of horsebacking.

By the time Jed finished supper and went out front into the settling night, he was beginning to believe his imagination was running away with him. While he was standing there, a light came slowly to life over in the jailhouse.

He went over. Charley was stoking the little iron stove and only looked around long enough to satisfy himself about the identity of his visitor. As he dropped a lucifer into the mixture of paper and fat wood and closed the stove's door, he faced around and told Jed Ames that he looked as solemn as an owl.

Jed sank into a chair. "There's another stranger come along. We met him up where we was cuttin' wood. Said his name's Liam Baxter, an' he's from Wyoming."

Charley went to his desk, sat down, and rocked back. "Not that damned cache again, Jed?"

Ames told the constable of the conversation between Baxter

and Jim Neely. He also mentioned the tied-down gun, and he finally had to admit that the man from Wyoming was likable enough with a quick smile and an easy way about him.

Charley's private thought made him say: "We're gettin' faunchy about strangers. Hell, they do pass through every few days."

"But they don't ask questions like this one asked," Jed retorted, beginning to feel a little annoyed. "Why would he want to know how to get to the Terwilliger place an' what Amelia Thatcher's name was?" This, at least, struck a cord with the lawman. He rocked forward and leaned on the desk. Before he could speak, his friend had another two-bits' worth to say. "The more I thought on it, Charley, the more it seemed to me a range rider, passin' through, wouldn't give a damn about the Terwilliger place or its new owner. Would he?"

Charley briefly hung fire before speaking. "Where is this feller, Jed?"

"I got no idea. Maybe at the hotel. Maybe at Cork's place."

"What's he look like?"

"Shorter'n me, sort of nice-lookin', pleasant, laughs a lot, wears the finest pair of silver inlaid spurs I ever saw. You can't miss him, Charley. He's friendly as a tan yard pup."

After the harness maker departed, Charley put on his hat and started a systematic round of the town, but there was no sign of Liam Baxter. Cork recalled the man, mainly because he drank beer instead of hard liquor and also because he was friendly and inquisitive. He seemed to know something about the Terwilliger place and had told Cork he was on his way down to New Mexico to escape the north country's hard winters.

Later, Charley bedded down thinking about this latest stranger, but lost very little sleep about it. He'd hunt up Liam Baxter in the morning.

He got too late a start. Jim Neely told Charley the range man had left town about sunrise. He had joked with the liveryman but had not said what his destination was.

"Which way did he ride?" Charley wondered.

"Northwest."

Charley's intention, when he discovered the stranger had left town, was to saddle up and hunt for him, but, after what Neely had said, he returned to his office to fire up the stove before crossing over to the café. Another damned cache hunter as sure as God had made sour apples. For some reason they had proliferated like weeds this summer and autumn. More had come to Charley's attention lately than in all the years he'd been in Cache Valley.

At dusk Jim Neely appeared at the jailhouse to express worry about the stranger, and all Charley could say was that, since the man rode his own horse, there was nothing for him to worry about. The answer he got was short and worrisome.

"He told me he'd be back before sundown. You don't expect he got hurt, do you?"

Although Charley had not met Liam Baxter as yet, from what he'd heard of the man he was too seasoned to get into a situation he couldn't get out of, and that is what he told Neely.

Later, with the little stove crackling, Charley had a premonition. Maybe Liam Baxter hadn't gone up to Cache Cañon. After all, he'd asked questions about Amelia and the Terwilliger place. As he set the stove's damper and blew out the hanging lamp, he told himself because of his interest in Amelia Thatcher he was imagining things and that, furthermore, if Baxter had gone to the Terwilliger place, Amelia had hired men who could, and certainly would, take care of anything untoward that might happen out there. He went to bed annoyed with himself for allowing his thoughts to be so heavily influenced by concern for Amelia. He would, however, locate Liam Baxter the next day.

The following morning Charley was in the café when Jim Neely came in and sat down next to him. In a relieved tone he said the stranger's horse was dozing in its stall when he had arrived to do his morning chores.

Charley had a leisurely breakfast before going over to the jailhouse. He hadn't been there but a short time when Lewis Boles walked in, handed him a sealed envelope, and left without saying a word.

The enclosed note was brief. Would Charley ride out to the ranch today? He reread the note, pocketed it, and went to the livery barn for his animal. This time Neely hardly spoke. He did not even, as was his custom, go out back and see which way the constable rode. If he had, it might have added another note to local gossip. Charley rode almost due west, the direction of the Terwilliger ranch.

It was another of those crisp, cold, autumn mornings with one exception — the sun, which normally cast no warmth this time of year, was brilliantly high and dazzling. The nightlong frost melted swiftly, and, as the day progressed, it was almost like summer.

When Charley had the ranch yard in sight, the riders were heading out in a bunch. They separated, each man, or two men, riding in a different direction. An outfit as large as the Terwilliger place required considerable saddlebacking, more so in autumn when cattle drifted a lot, seeking something other than dry graze. If they saw Charley in the sun-bright distance, they gave no indication of it.

Instead of tying up in front of the barn, Charley rode across the yard and tied up at the rack to one side of the porch steps. Amelia came out before he had made the horse fast. He guessed she had seen his approach from a window. She neither smiled nor greeted him as she held the door open. In the parlor, where a brisk fire was burning, she got Charley a cup of black coffee and sat opposite him as she said: "There's something I want to tell you. I would have told you eventually."

Charley loosened his coat. It was hot in the house.

"I knew a man in Cheyenne. He came around a lot, and he was pleasant with a sense of humor . . . and he was not only very attentive, he was good-looking. Before my mother died, she told me he'd make a good husband. We were engaged."

Charley was expressionless as he listened. The only movement he made was to put the emptied coffee cup aside and drop his hat beside his chair.

"I liked him, but there were rumors that upset me."

Finally Charley spoke. "What kind of rumors?"

"For one thing it was said he was married and had abandoned his wife in Montana."

"Any way of telling whether it was the truth?" Charley asked.

Amelia blushed and avoided Charley's direct gaze when she answered. "It's nothing I'm proud of, Charley."

"There's things we all ain't proud of, Amelia."

"The telegrapher was the husband of a woman who was my best friend. He showed my friend a message he'd received from a town over in Idaho where there was a murder warrant out for the man."

Charley interrupted. "Liam Baxter?"

She gave a delayed reply. "You know about Liam?"

"No. I've been puttin' two an' two together while I been listenin' to you. Tell me somethin', Amelia. Why would a telegrapher over in Idaho send a message to a telegrapher in Cheyenne about Baxter?"

"Because someone up in Wyoming recognized him from Idaho, and the sheriff up there wired Idaho for more information. Charley, he was here last night."

Charley had to stand up and shrug out of his coat. Although the fire was diminishing, the parlor seemed to have become hotter. As he sat down again, he asked: "Where is he now?"

Amelia didn't know. "I made supper for him, and we visited. I offered a place at the bunkhouse, but he declined."

Charley gazed out a front wall window where the sun continued to warm the world with unseasonable heat. While gazing out the window, he inquired if Amelia knew anything about the killing in Idaho. She didn't, but she did know that Liam Baxter was said in Wyoming to be deadly with a six-gun. She did not mention where she'd heard that, nor did she have to. Charley had fleshed out his suspicions.

He asked if Baxter would return.

Amelia's answer was prompt. "He said he would. He said he'd heard up in Cheyenne that I'd inherited a big cow outfit. He said he was an experienced range boss."

"Did you tell him you already had one?"

"No. Charley, I was afraid of him. He was in most ways the man of charm and humor and warmth my mother had liked. She died before my close friend's husband could tell her about Liam's being wanted in Idaho. I was speechless when Liam knocked on my door. I wish you could have been here. I was frightened."

"Did he act like he knew it, Amelia?"

"No, I don't think so. We had supper, sat where you and I are sitting now, and recalled old times." She blushed again. "I told him he could stay overnight at the bunkhouse and went down to the barn with him when he saddled up to leave. His last words were that he liked the country down here, and he'd come see me again soon."

Amelia did the same thing when Charley left, but this time she only had to go as far as the tie rack in front of the porch. She watched the constable snug up his horse's cinch, and, before he mounted, she said: "If he comes back, Charley . . . ?"

From the saddle, while evening up his reins, the constable smiled downward. "There's a good chance he won't, Amelia. Not if he's in town when I get back."

This time the long trip back to Rock City seemed to Charley to take forever. What helped to make it seem that way was the constable's admission to himself that he was right taken with Amelia Thatcher.

Chapter Fifteen

TROUBLE COMING

In a lawman's line of work surprises could almost be said to occur on a daily basis, but for some reason Charley was not surprised when Jim Neely told him the "nice feller" who owned the muscled-up bay horse had ridden out so early the liveryman hadn't quite finished his morning chores.

"Rode north," Jim Neely reported.

Charley had to settle for that, even though north could be anywhere since he might have readily changed direction once out of town. In any event, the constable had a feeling Liam Baxter would be scouting up the Terwilliger range. Charley was firing up the office stove at the jailhouse when he pretty well reached a conclusion about the man from Wyoming, but it would take time to prove him right or wrong. In the meantime, he had to wait, which is what he did.

Up at the harness shop he and Jed exchanged cryptic ideas. Jed Ames had also done some soul searching about Liam Baxter, and, if Charley had repeated all that Amelia Thatcher had told him, Jed's suspicions would have firmed up. Charley did tell the harness maker about the telegraph information up in Cheyenne, and Jed was handing the constable a mug of black java when he said: "You get the feelin' this stranger ain't much different from them other ones?"

Charley had made that connection at the jailhouse. He raised the cup. The coffee was too hot, so he put the cup aside before answering. "Because he's a stranger? Maybe."

163

"I meant if he abandoned a wife an' is maybe wanted over in Idaho."

Charley got closer to the little stove. At the jailhouse he had reluctantly decided he had first to contact Cheyenne to find out where Baxter was wanted, then write the authorities over there, and he hated writing letters. In fact, he'd learned early that, when a person wrote a letter, they invariably got one back that required more writing.

The constable spent the rest of the day at the jailhouse cleaning, oiling, and reloading the array of weapons from the gun rack. While cleaning guns was a good time in which to ponder, and Charley did his share of that, not only about the man from Wyoming but also about the woman who was from Wyoming.

He had supper across the street at the café. It was while he was eating that another diner, Lex Morton, had to shift position to accommodate his wooden leg while he looked out the window. "There goes that newcomer," he said.

Charley twisted around to look. Liam Baxter was almost beyond the range of sight, but Charley had seen enough to recognize him when he saw him again. He faced forward again and finished his supper without haste. It was early dusk when he left the café.

Down at the livery barn Jim Neely was gone. His hosteler was forking feed and doling out rolled barley from a coffee can. He acknowledged the constable instantly and called a greeting. Charley answered and entered the harness room while the hosteler continued his chores.

There were a number of saddles on wall racks. There were also several sets of harness, mostly with chain tugs, but there were some lighter California harness. Charley had no difficulty locating the right saddle. It was still warm. He rummaged the saddle pockets, finding nothing out of the ordinary and including several tins of sardines, the range man's last resort — not because range men like sardines, but because the tins were flat and required little space.

As he was rummaging, the hosteler came in and stopped to stare. Charley mumbled something innocuous and departed. Later, while the constable was up at Finney's Pleasure Palace, the hosteler told Jim Neely what he had caught the lawman doing, and the liveryman, whose widowed life consisted of dull, predictable repetition, could only speculate.

At Cork's place the customary patrons had been arriving for an hour or so. These included a number of range men. Until Charley remembered that this was Friday, he had wondered about so many ranch hands being at the bar.

Bob Scott, a Terwilliger range man Charley hadn't recognized at first, was at the bar. He turned and said: "We're gettin' our share of visitors lately, Constable." When Charley disinterestedly nodded, while watching Cork squint his eyes nearly closed to avoid cigar smoke while he filled the constable's jolt glass, Scott continued speaking. "Me 'n' Lew was huntin' for tender-footed bulls some miles west of Cache Cañon when we come onto a husky-built feller. He said his name was Baxter, that he was from up north, an' because he liked the country, he was ridin' around to get familiar with it."

Cork moved along, and Charley turned toward Scott. He asked about Baxter.

The Terwilliger rider smiled. "Pleasant feller. He helped us hunt bulls, which we never found."

Charley considered his jolt glass for a few moments before dropping its contents straight down. When he looked around, Scott had moved farther along the bar where other riders were congregating. He was about ready to head for his room at the hotel when someone entered, and Bob Scott called: "Howdy, Baxter. I'll stand the first round."

The husky man smiled broadly as he angled in the direction of the range men, who accepted him without visible reservation, which was neither common nor uncommon. Range men were usually not welcome among townsfolk because they were notorious for being troublesome.

Charley had plenty of time to study the man from Wyoming, particularly his spurs and the unorthodox way he prevented his six-gun from getting jarred out of its holster. With the passage of time the range men became less noisy and more concerned with drinking. One thing was clear to Charley. This was Friday evening. They had two more days to loaf and were getting a fair start. So far, none was drunk, but if custom had anything to do with it, that was simply a matter of time.

He wanted to strike up a casual conversation with Liam Baxter, but as time passed that did not appear as even a remote possibility. Whether the man from Wyoming knew who the constable was or not — and it was possible he hadn't seen the badge — he was perfectly at home among the range men.

Cork came down the bar to lean forward and say softly: "If you're goin' to call him, don't do it in here. There's too many of them."

Charley nodded and continued to lean in place. He had plenty of time. Eventually either Baxter or the range men would leave. As it happened, they left together. Two of them had to be steered in the direction of the street. With their departure Finney's regulars, all townsmen, breathed a sigh of relief. One man, a corral-yard hosteler, said: "I thought I knew 'em all, but that one with the fancy spurs I never seen before."

No one picked up on that. For the most part Cork Finney's customers were either single men or those who were married and habitually made for the saloon for their night caps. Charley went out into settling night and watched the range men leave town on horseback, two on each side of the unsteady men.

Liam Baxter waved, several riders waved back, and then Baxter turned. His expression did not change at sight of the large, solemn man wearing the badge. He said: "There'll be some boys sticking their heads in a water trough come morning."

Charley was unimpressed by the shorter man's easy geniality. Without having met Baxter, he'd heard enough about him. He addressed him quietly. "You're from Cheyenne?"

This time Baxter's expression of geniality slowly faded before he nodded. "Cheyenne . . . an' other places."

The constable nodded. "My name's Charley Bent."

Baxter nodded without offering his hand. "Nice town," he told the lawman.

Charley added a little to that. "Nice valley, nice folks . . . Mister Baxter, save us both some trouble. Stay away from Amelia Thatcher."

This time the surprise showed. "Her 'n' me been friends a long time, Constable. She's the first one I hunted up when I got here."

Charley said: "I know. Do us both a favor. Stay away from her."

The husky man's expression showed a faint, almost imperceptible smile. "Well, now, Constable, I don't think what's between Amelia an' me is anyone's business but ours."

Charley watched a solitary horseman lope past. The man threw a wave, and Charley waved back. Then he gazed dispassionately at Liam Baxter. "I'm makin' it my business."

This time Baxter's retort had no shred of geniality. "Mister, Amelia 'n' me was engaged. Far as I know, there's no law that can make me stay away from her." Baxter put his head slightly to one side, considered the larger and older man briefly, then added: "You a single man, Constable?" When Charley did not reply, Baxter's slight, humorless smile reappeared. "You're

167

wastin' your time," he said. "Her 'n' me been real close for three years."

Cork inadvertently came through the spindle doors to fling a pail of greasy water into the street. He stopped dead still when he saw who the constable was facing. He turned back, carrying the unemptied pail. He usually emptied his water pails out the back, anyway. Liam Baxter used this interlude to cross the street and walk in the direction of the hotel.

Cork peeked out now, saw Baxter retreating, and spoke in a lowered voice. "You mind that one, Charley. In my business, if you don't learn much else, you sure Lord get to know people, an' that one's real honest to God trouble four ways from the middle."

Charley returned to the jailhouse to douse the lamp and close up for the night. The front door lock still didn't work, not since the lynching. There was no locksmith in Rock City, or any place close by, but the town carpenter could repair the door, and Charley made a mental note to get another lock.

He spent a half hour in his room wondering whether he had done right or wrong in warning Baxter to stay away from Amelia. Maybe he should have let it slide. But she was afraid of the man, and, from what Charley now knew, her fear was justified.

He bedded down, still querying himself about what he'd done, and of one thing he was certain. Liam Baxter now knew that Constable Bent hadn't laid down the law to him just for the hell of it. Baxter hadn't impressed Charley as a fool. He would figure out, if he hadn't already done it, that the local lawman's concern arose from his personal feeling about Frank Terwilliger's heir. Charley didn't drop off to sleep until he told himself that he hadn't just alienated Liam Baxter. He had done it in a manner that would ensure trouble for Amelia, which it had been his intention to avoid.

He awakened from a troubled sleep before sunup, and, as had happened before, Charley was the caféman's first customer. Also, as before, the caféman read the constable's expression correctly and, after feeding him, did not come out of his cooking area until he heard the street door close.

There were clouds gathering, white except for their underbellies. There was a cold breeze coming out of the north. Autumn was yielding to what came next. Charley stoked up the jailhouse stove and stood at the small, front, barred window, looking out. His mood matched the weather.

Later he went across the street to the Emporium. The mail that had arrived on the early southbound stage had been sorted in a timely fashion. A letter had confirmed receipt of one Bill Morgan, alias Bill Smith, in Brownsville, Texas. A five-hundred-dollar reward, which had been offered for his capture, would follow. It marked the end of that business, anyhow. He thought about riding out to the Terwilliger place to tell Amelia about his meeting with Liam Baxter. He might have done it, but time passed and then Sam Brennen, in an unpleasant temper, came in and slammed the door as he glared at the lawman.

Charley stifled a sigh. "Storm comin'," he said. He went to the desk and sat down.

Brennen made his little sniffing sound of irritability. He stood wide-legged, glaring. "Well, while you're settin' in here where it's warm, another of my stages has been stopped."

Charley made no attempt this time to stifle the sigh as he leaned back away from the desk. "When, Sam?"

"This mornin', early. The southbound. In danged near the same place. The stage has come back. You sure that stage robber you sent to Texas didn't get loose?"

"Smith? You saw the irons on him, Sam."

"That don't have to mean he ain't back, Charley."

"Oh, yes, it does. I got confirmation from Brownsville just

169

today. Besides, if he'd've escaped, you would have heard about it all along the line."

"Reckon that's right, Constable, but Smith or no Smith, the stage has been robbed."

"What was stolen?"

"No mail was touched, an' there was no express shipment, but they had the passengers an' driver line up. Robbed 'em all, down to their boots. The passengers are mad, Charley. They're down at my office. If you got off your butt, you could maybe run him down. It wasn't that long ago."

"You said *they*. If it had been Smith, it would have been just one man. Which was it, Sam, one man or more than one?"

"One man is what the whip and the passengers saw. But that don't mean there wasn't more watchin' from hiding, does it?"

"I'll ride out," Charley said, rising, "but first I want to talk to the driver and passengers." He turned to get his coat.

"The driver's Jeff Butler. C'mon, they're all down at my office. I figure I'll take 'em over to Cork's before I send 'em out again."

Charley put on his hat and, together with Brennen, hiked over to the stage office at the corral yard. As Brennen had said, the whip, Jeff Butler, and the three passengers, were congregated in the office, keeping warm. The passengers, all men, two drummers and a mining engineer, wanted to talk, but the constable addressed Butler first. The driver was a thin, almost cadaverous-looking individual. Charley wanted a description of the highwayman.

"Average size feller, maybe in his forties," Butler reported. "His face was pretty well covered, but me 'n' Carter, that drummer over there, was struck by somethin' uncommon. He had the finest pair of silver spurs we'd ever seen."

Carter nodded in agreement, and Charley loosened a little.

170

"How did he wear the tie-down over his pistol, Jeff?"

Butler looked pained. "Constable, when a man's lookin' into the barrel of a cocked hand gun, he don't see much else."

After talking with each of the passengers, who confirmed the stage driver's description but could add little more, Charley left the corral yard. He promised to do what he could to apprehend the highwayman. In the meantime, claims for money and personal items lost in the robbery were to be filled out and left with Sam Brennen.

The cold was no longer being driven by wind, but that did little to mitigate the constable's discomfort as he rode south under an increasingly dark and unfriendly sky. He had no difficulty finding where the coach had been stopped. As Sam Brennen had said, it was close to the place the other coach had been stopped. It could have been a coincidence, but, as Charley sat his saddle studying the countryside, he decided the entire area roundabout was ideal for stopping stages, or other vehicles for that matter.

Picking up shod horse marks was less obvious. For one thing the wind had pretty well scoured the road down to hardpan, but on the east side of the road, where there were trees and more underbrush, picking up the highwayman's route of escape was less difficult, thanks to the tough sage, thornpin, and chaparral. In open places the wind had scoured the ground, but among the underbrush, which it had been unable to break through, there were tracks.

Charley rode slowly and hunched to one side. If he had expected the tracks to veer off more toward the northwest and Cache Cañon, they did not veer off. The sign went almost due north in the direction of Rock City, and that troubled him. Highwaymen left the scene of a robbery in the direction of timbered or rocky country. He had tracked his share, and this was the first time he was on the track of a highwayman heading for a town. Charley rummaged his memory for townsmen who could have robbed the stage. While Rock City, like all towns, had its share of questionable individuals, the closer Charley got back to where he had started out, the harder it got for him to believe the highwayman — or highwaymen, although the tracks did not indicate more than one man — would be foolish enough to head for home, if, indeed, he were from town. The tracks only altered course where the rider had been compelled to circle wide around huge boulders, forbidding stands of underbrush, or the occasional tree. Charley had town in sight with smoke rising from stoves and fireplaces before he began to think ahead about where the highwayman had gone, where he might be hiding. He lost the sign when the tracks headed into the road just below Rock City.

Charley rode along the main thoroughfare with a rising wind at his back, saw that the stage had pulled out again, although he had missed seeing it, probably because he had been following those tracks around some rock outcropping. He turned in at the livery barn to care for his horse, and was neither interrupted nor helped by the liveryman for the best of all reasons. Jim Neely was in the saddle room near a popping stove. Livery barn runways were made to order for wind. They were wide and open at both ends.

Charley stalled and fed his horse. He did not so much as look in the direction of the saddle room as he left. He bucked a head wind all the way to the jailhouse, where the room was frigid and there were no coals, so he had to start all over again, unmindful that outside those monstrous cloud galleons with the threatening undersides were very close to passing directly overhead.

He had shed his coat and gloves and was facing the stove with both hands extended when Sam Brennen came in. He had a knitted cap pulled down over his ears and was bundled into an oversize, bearskin coat in which generations of moths had lived. He removed a pair of gloves and went to stand beside the larger man, hands extended when he asked the question Charley anticipated.

"You find the son-of-a-bitch?"

"All I can tell you," Charley replied, "is that his tracks led back here to town."

Brennen looked up. "Here? In town?"

Charley nodded.

"You mean that bastard lives among us, Charley?"

"What I'm sayin', Sam, is that I tracked him from down yonder almost arrow straight to town."

The corral-yard boss was speechless, but that was something that neither happened often nor for more than short periods. "I don't believe it!" he finally exclaimed.

Charley was thawed out by this time and went to his desk chair, to sit there eyeing the shorter man. When Brennen turned, his expression was stubbornly unbelieving. "It was that bastard, Smith, sure as I'm standin' here, an' you know it."

Charley didn't argue. "All right, it was Smith. Now tell me, Sam, why a man known hereabouts to be an outlaw, and who likely knew what happened to Shokely, would do anything as stupid as to head for Rock City after he robbed a stage?"

Sam had no answer for that. He stood with his back to the stove, steadily regarding the constable. Eventually he said: "It'd maybe be someone who knew when the southbound would be passin' there, wouldn't it?"

Charley shrugged without speaking, which was just as well. The corral-yard boss's mind was working overtime. He wouldn't have heard the constable if he had spoken.

"It's got to be one of my yard men," Brennen opined. "Or maybe someone I fired, who used to work at the yard. Someone who'd know the schedules. You're plumb positive he come

173

back here after stoppin' the coach?"

Charley did as he'd done before. He nodded his head without saying a word.

News of the robbery had spread fast. The fact that the three unhappy victims of the robbery had remained in town for a time had helped this process. Charley was encountered by close to a dozen indignant townsfolk. All he could tell them was what he had told Sam Brennen, but Brennen's handiwork was evident in some of the stories Charley heard. One of these stories had it that Sam Brennen had visited the Emporium to find out who was in arrears with an account, in other words, who was desperate enough to rob a stage. Charley grimaced to himself after he heard that. When George Crittenden had run the store, he was forever complaining that half the folks in Rock City were in arrears.

Chapter Sixteen

A COLD RIDE AND A NEAR MISS

The wind was howling. Charley heard it rattle the only window in his room and went deeper under the blankets. He did not hear the rain until he awakened shortly before sunrise — except that this morning there was no sun. It would appear later, after the storm had passed, but before that the townsfolk remained inside, checking for leaky roofs and also staying warm. Despite the wind, if there had been enough light, it would have been possible to tell from the tattered clouds that the real force of the wind was miles overhead. It was that invisible high wind that carried the storm clouds southwest, and by midday Rock City had got all the storm it would get, for a while anyway, and it was enough. The town had been thoroughly soaked.

The main street was a morass. Merchants laid planks across it. By this time Cork Finney's Pleasure Palace, like other business establishments and the jailhouse, had lights showing, but there was no foot traffic until the sun shown, and while people appeared, unless they had to cross on the duck boards, there was not much activity. Only the stockmen rejoiced. Rainfall any time was very welcome, even with winter on the way, because the ground absorbed the water, which it did not do when it was frozen and the snow came.

Lex Morton, stomping along on his wooden leg, came to the jailhouse, cursing the mud and wrapped in an old buffalo coat that reached from his bony shoulders to his ankles. A gray muffler nearly hid his face, and both hands were encased in oversize bearskin gloves. He went to stand by the stove without offering a greeting, and, when the heat was felt to be adequate, he loosened the heavy, old coat and put his back to the stove. He was facing the constable when he said: "You hear about the stage robbery?"

Charley stretched back in his desk chair. By now everyone from hell to breakfast had heard about the stage being stopped. "Yesterday," he told Morton, and leaned forward to ask the old man a question. "You just heard about it?"

Morton gimped to a chair, eased down gingerly so that his wooden extremity would be straight out, and made a little teasing smile. "Ray Kemp told me this mornin'. I went up to see if he'd eaten yet. Sometimes him 'n' me share breakfast. Ray's down with the scourge. I made us both a meal and had to spoon it down him. He's runnin' a fever 'n' all. You got to remember Ray's gettin' on in years."

"I'm sorry to hear Ray's sick," Charley commiserated. "Is that what you came to tell me?"

"No. You familiar with a feller named Baxter?"

Charley nodded.

"Well, while I was feedin' Ray, he told me Baxter come in last night, smellin' real strong of horse sweat."

Charley had made a mistake last night. He should have visited the livery barn. It was too late now. "Did Ray say anythin' else?" he asked.

"Only that he'd heard the talk of that highwayman comin' to town, an' that Sam Brennen thinks it's got to be someone who's got it in for him." The old man smiled slyly again. "Ray 'n' me agreed that could damn' well be two-thirds of the local folks."

Charley leaned forward in his chair. The strong scent of horse sweat didn't have to mean anything. The same two-thirds of local folks Lex Morton had mentioned would smell of horse sweat on almost any given day.

176

"Ray said he met Baxter in the hallway, and always before Baxter took time to talk and seemed relaxed. Last night he didn't even nod to Ray, just went into his room and closed the door."

Charley thanked Morton for the information. It wasn't long after he had gone that Lewis Boles came to the jailhouse. He did as he'd done before. He greeted Charley, handed him a sealed envelope, and departed without saying another word. Today he had a reason for being abrupt, if he needed one. It was a long, cold ride from the Terwilliger Ranch to Rock City. A man got uncomfortably in need of something to kindle a fire in his stomach.

The note from Amelia asked Charley to come out as soon as he could. Liam Baxter had showed up again the previous day, and she felt in danger. Charley had already decided Baxter's purpose for exploring the Terwilliger spread was to get an idea of how large Amelia's inheritance was and how many cattle there were. What struck Charley was the clear and obvious fear in Amelia when she had written the appeal for help.

He put the note in his drawer, put another paper in his pocket, and reached for his hat. Somewhere, either on the Terwilliger range or perhaps in town, he would find Baxter. He was not enthusiastic about making the ride out to the Terwilliger place, not over miles of muddy soil with the tail end of the earlier wind still hugging the ground, so he went up to the hotel.

He didn't expect to see Ray Kemp. After all, Lex Morton had reported that the hotelman was ailing. Charley tried three doors. While all were unlocked and clearly untenanted, when he tried the next door, the one nearest the kitchen, it was locked. He could have gone looking for Ray Kemp. Instead, he lifted the latch as far as it would go and leaned his entire weight against the panel. It quivered but did not yield until

177

Charley had leaned twice more, the last time with his feet braced.

The door opened.

His search was a disappointment. There was nothing in the room that indicated Liam Baxter was the tenant. There was one set of muddy boots, a spare set of clothing, shaving utensils, and two blankets that from their crumpled appearance were part of a bedroll.

Leaving the hotel, Charley checked both sides of the main street without finding Baxter. Only in one place had he even been seen, that was at the café. The caféman said a stranger answering Baxter's description had eaten there and had paid for an extra meal to be carried with him in a saddle pocket. That was all.

Something nagged at Charley about making the ride out to the Terwilliger place. Up until now he had been reluctant about it. Now there was no reluctance.

While his horse was being rigged out at the livery stable, Charley returned to the jailhouse for his rider's coat, the gloves that went with it, and an itchy woolen muffler. When he returned to the barn, he asked Jim Neely if the muscled-up, short-backed horse was in one of the corrals, and got a brusque reply from the liveryman. "No, sir. The stranger brought it in yesterday, late, sweatin' like it'd been rode hard. He gave me a cartwheel to walk it until it was cooled an' to rub it down good, stall it, and give it extra rolled barley. When I come in this mornin', it was gone. So was the Miles City saddle."

Charley did not push his animal. In most places the ground yielded only slightly, but there were other places where the horse sank, which made each step harder to take. And there was no reason for haste, at least not the kind of haste Charley had made on previous trips. On those rides he hadn't been thinking of Liam Baxter.

178

He rationalized as he rode. If Baxter wasn't in town, and if he'd ridden out early, he'd certainly had a destination. After the recent storm and the biting cold which had settled in its place, no one went horsebacking for pleasure. It bothered Charley more now than it had when he'd warned Baxter to stay away from Amelia that the man had visited the Terwilliger place again.

The constable had to cross an icy creek where his horse did not quite balk but did require firm convincing that the creek had to be crossed. On the other side he saw a wolf jump from among the creek willows and flee. Charley could have shot him. The reason he didn't was not the reason that would have made a cowman hesitate. The wolf was old, thin, and ran with a noticeable limp. His kind followed cattle, particularly cows heavy with calf. They would kill newborns, but their main diet was afterbirth. Wolves were anathema to stockmen any time, but particularly in early spring which was calving time. Charley pushed past the willows and watched the old wolf who seemed to know exactly how far to run before he was out of gun range. That, or he was too weak and crippled to continue running.

Charley watched the wolf because there was nothing else to hold his interest. Very abruptly the wolf, which had been heading for a deep arroyo, veered hard to his right and raced along the rim of the gully. Ten seconds later Charley heard the gunshot and felt the slug pass his right ear close enough to roil the air. He left the saddle in a leap, turned his horse sideways, and drew his Colt, for which the range was too great, and waited. There was no second shot. He remained behind the horse, watching and waiting. He saw nothing until the sound of a rider gave him an indication in which direction the bushwhacker was heading.

As long as the ambusher remained in the deep arroyo, Charley could not see him, but neither could the bushwhacker

179

see Charley. He mounted and reined on an angling course in the direction of the arroyo, but the ambusher had too long a head start. Where he eventually burst out of the arroyo in plain sight, he was far beyond the range of any pistol. He was also moving too fast, widening the distance between himself and the constable, for Charley to get a good look at him.

The constable resumed his ride toward the Terwilliger Ranch. Any lawman who has followed his trade any length of time makes enemies. In direct proportion to the length of time he wears a badge, the number of enemies increases. This may have been what had led to the attempt on his life.

As he neared the Terwilliger ranch buildings, there was spiraling smoke rising from the chimney of the ranch house and also from the stove pipe of the bunkhouse. Charley crossed the ranch yard and dismounted at the barn. He hesitated momentarily to care for his animal before leaving the barn to cross toward the ranch house.

Amelia was surprised when she opened the door. Behind her in the fireplace in the south wall was a blazing fire. Charley shucked his coat and dropped it while mentioning her note.

She looked the same except that she did not smile. She took him to the fireplace, left to go get hot coffee. When she returned, she said: "Liam was here again."

"When?" Charley asked.

"Last night before the rain." Amelia's tone was curt. "He told me you'd warned him to stay away from me. Charley . . . ?"

The constable nodded and lifted his coffee cup. "I did tell him to stay away from you."

"He said . . . he didn't like the way you spoke. He said . . . he accused me of leading you on."

Charley put the cup on the mantle and faced her, almost smiling. "If that's what you been doin', I'm real glad. Were you doin' that, Amelia?"

She moved the conversation in a more serious direction. "He told me, if I saw you again, he'd kill you."

Charley moved away from the hot fire, sank into a chair, and decided not to tell her that someone had, indeed, tried to kill him. He said: "Let me tell you what I've figured. He's been exploring Terwilliger range."

Amelia sat down across from him. "I know, Lew Boles. . . ."

"By now he's got a fair idea of how many cattle you run which'll give him an idea of how much land you control." Charley hunched forward with both hands clasped between his knees. "If he's what I think he might be, Amelia, he's not goin' to ride away from a woman he was engaged to, especially now that she's got a big cow outfit that's worth a sizable bit of money."

They sat briefly in silence, the only sound coming from the stone fireplace. Eventually she spoke. "Do you think I should move to town? The woman at the general store offered to let me stay with her any time I wanted to."

Charley was thinking of something he'd heard at the saloon when he replied: "You said she makes you uncomfortable."

"They both do, Bertha and the clerk. I could stay at that hotel."

Charley said quietly: "Baxter's got a room there." He rose to go closer to the fire. Then he faced around. "You'd ought to tell your riders about Baxter. Not to pick a fight with him, just to keep close if he's seen out yonder or here at the ranch. They're loyal to the brand. I know that for a fact." He did not say how he knew, or he would have had to tell her the full story of the fight in Cache Cañon.

As though she derived a sense of safety from Charley's presence, Amelia changed the subject. "Did I give you back that map of the Cache Cañon country?"

Charley nodded. He had the map in his pocket now. He

was willing to pursue a different subject, so he repeated what was an old story to him. There was no cache. He knew that people had been hunting for it since before he came into the country. They had dug and rolled rocks, had looked for unusual formations of stones, even blazes on trees, and no one had ever found anything.

She got up and made them Irish coffees. Later, as she sipped hers, she told him she neither liked the taste of whiskey nor the confusion it caused her, and he smiled. He had been a whiskey drinker since his teens. In all that time he could count on the fingers of one hand how many times he'd actually been drunk.

She asked if the cold ride from town had made him hungry. He told her that it certainly had and rose to watch her leave the parlor in the direction of the kitchen. Dinner was in the oven. He resumed his chair — the faint scent of lavender lingered — until the sound of her working in the kitchen made Charley wish he had a cigar. He would have enjoyed one in this setting, but the few Cork Finney had insisted he take over the years were in the bottom drawer of his desk at the jailhouse.

Amelia then called, asking Charley if he would please fetch in some stove wood. He got back into his coat and brought in an armload to fill the kitchen woodbox. He also went out back in order to replenish the split red fir logs for the fireplace in the parlor.

He'd been in the Terwilliger house several times over the years, but it was so different now, he scarcely recalled how it had been when the brothers had lived here. For one thing, in those former days the place had a sour smell. Now it was not only immaculate, but that faint lavender aroma seemed to be everywhere.

Amelia fed him what appeared to be one of the largest chickens he had ever seen. It was, she told him, a goose. One of the riders had shot two and had given her one. Charley should have known. Geese were dark meat. Chickens had breasts of white meat. It was odd how a stone sober man could make the mistakes Charley Bent tended to make when he was with Amelia Thatcher.

Later, when he was shrugging again into his coat, he asked her a pointblank question. "Amelia, ain't it sort of lonesome bein' a widow lady?"

She answered while they were facing one another at the door. "It's very lonesome, Charley."

"Well, ma'am, I have a friend in town. He's the saddle 'n' harness maker. Makes a decent living, is single, and a real good man."

She stiffened while he was speaking, leaned forward, picked up his hat, thrust it at him, and closed the door firmly after he was outside.

Chapter Seventeen

OR HER!

Charley returned to town by a more southerly route than the one he had taken on the way out. He wasn't too seriously concerned about the bushwhacker both because of the difference in the trail he had chosen and also because the ride back to Rock City was being made in darkness.

The town had bedded down by the time Charley reached the livery barn where the night hosteler came from the harness room, rubbing his eyes, but pleasant in his manner. The constable had little to say, and, after Charley left, the hosteler consoled himself with the thought that lawmen were not talkative by nature.

Up at the hotel Charley roused the ailing hotelman from his bed. Ray Kemp, perhaps because he was under the weather, seemed more resigned than annoyed by the intrusion. He stated in answer to Charley's question that Liam Baxter was staying in room number 4. "He ain't in there now, though," Kemp said. "Leastwise, I didn't see him come in before I turned down the parlor lamp for the night."

Charley made his own inspection. It was the same room he had looked in earlier, and Ray Kemp had been right. The bed hadn't been slept in.

The constable went to his own room and was in the act of preparing to bed down when the sound of a shod horse, traveling southward, caught his interest. It was a dark night, and all he could make out from his window was the silhouette of a solitary horseman. He could not see

184

well enough to identify the rider.

On his way back to sit on the edge of his bed, Charley had an unpleasant thought. If that had not been Baxter in the darkened street, riding in the direction of the livery barn, and if Baxter was the one who had tried to bushwhack Charley, afterward waiting until Charley left the Terwilliger place, Amelia might now be at his mercy. There was a reason for doubt, however. If Baxter had been the bushwhacker — and Charley was inclined to believe he had been — he could have shot Charley out of the saddle when he rode out of the Terwilliger ranch yard to return to Rock City. But then, as Charley had surmised, he might have been lying in wait along the same trail Charley had taken out to see Amelia, in which case he would have been frustrated in his vigil. If Baxter had been that rider, heading toward the livery stable, Amelia would be safe. If he weren't . . . ? Well, there were Lewis Boles and the other Terwilliger ranch hands.

He went to bed balancing these thoughts. Shortly before falling asleep, Charley accepted the premise that, if Baxter had really wanted to kill him, he could easily have done it in the Terwilliger ranch yard or perhaps soon after he left it. He speculated briefly about staying awake until he heard boot steps in the hallway, but fell asleep after that notion had only barely surfaced.

In the morning, after cleaning up out at the wash house, Charley went to the front of the hotel and stood a while, watching Rock City come to life. His normal routine was to cross the main street southward to the café, but this morning he did not cross over. Instead, he walked the full distance to the livery barn. Baxter's muscled-up horse was not there, and Jim Neely, who was in the act of trundling a wheelbarrow from stall to stall, cleaning out dung, reported that to his knowledge neither Liam Baxter nor his animal had come in during the night.

Charley went to breakfast. The café was moderately full. Heat from the cooking area clouded the street window, and conversation was in full swing. It did not abate when the constable walked in. The general speculation concerned the highwayman that Sam Brennen claimed had to be someone local.

Even the caféman had an opinion which he leaned across the counter to confide to Charley. "Only feller to fit Brennen's description would be" — and, here, the slovenly man leaned close enough to whisper — "Andy Buck!"

Charley finished eating, shelled out silver coins, and went out into the early morning chill. If the caféman knew anything, which he obviously didn't, he would have heard by now Sam Brennen's other suspicion — that the highwayman had been the outlaw extradited to Texas in chains. While crossing toward the jailhouse, it occurred to Charley that the reason Sam perhaps hadn't spread this rumor was because of what Charley had told him. It couldn't have been Smith. Because Sam really had to accept what Charley had told him about Smith, he was now probably convinced the highwayman was someone in town, possibly someone who had incurred Brennen's enmity. Sam should have shown better sense than to have mentioned something like that. He had to know he lacked a lot of being Rock City's favorite inhabitant.

The jailhouse was cold. Charley whittled kindling, wadded paper into a crumple, shoved the aggregate into the stove, and dropped in a lucifer. A burst of smoke came out before he got the door closed. It never took long for the office to get warm.

Charley was shuffling through papers on his desk, most of which consisted of wanted dodgers and unanswered correspondence, when Jed Ames walked in, looking very serious. As he

186

sank into a chair, he said: "Baxter's at the saloon." Before Charley could react, the harness maker added: "His horse is tied out in the back alley."

For a long moment the two men regarded each other. The only sound was of someone rattling past in a wagon whose axles hadn't been greased in a long time. Jed shoved up to his feet. He had been accumulating his doubts about the stranger from Wyoming for some time. Now he asked if Baxter had been at the hotel last night. When the constable said he hadn't, Jed made it to the door before he spoke again. "Put it together, Charley. He don't like you. Why, I got no idea, but how come a man would tie his horse in a back alley instead of out front at a tie rack, an' why would he be buildin' up dutch courage in the mornin' at Cork's place unless he was fixin' to get troublesome? He'd never leave town if he used a gun, an' his horse was tied out front. Charley, you got some idea why he don't like you?"

Charley answered: "Amelia Thatcher. He knew her up in Cheyenne. She's scairt of him. I told him to stay away from her."

Jed made a small, humorless smile. "Then, I'd say he's got reason."

After Jed went out, Charley rose slowly, dropped on his hat, lifted out his sidearm, spun the cylinder, set the trigger at half cock, and left the jailhouse himself. The sun was climbing. People, on both sides of the street, were too concerned with their own business to glance over where the constable stood. There wasn't a cloud in the sky. It would be another sparkling clear, warm, autumn day. There wouldn't be many more.

The duckboards were gone. It was now possible to cross over the main street without going ankle deep in mud, but the ground was still somewhat damp. Lex Morton, coming through the vacant but overgrown space beside the jailhouse, was mumbling curses to himself and asking for the thousandth time why the men who made wooden legs always had to taper the damned things until they were small and round at the bottom. Anyone with the sense God gave a goose should know peg legs sank past the ankle in moist earth, not to mention soil that had recently gone through a rain storm.

When he reached the plank walk, he paused to skive off the mud. While doing this, he saw Charley. "Mornin', Constable. I picked up a silver cartwheel yestiddy evenin'." He dug out the silver coin and held it on his palm. "I'll stand you to breakfast, if you ain't already et."

Charley did not look around. He said he had already eaten and slowly turned. As long as he'd known Lex Morton, the fellow had survived on handouts and an occasional stolen chicken. In a fashion, folks looked after him. Otherwise, he would have starved. Morton saw the way Charley was eyeing the silver dollar. "I didn't steal it."

"You found it?" Charley asked.

"No, sir. Last night, when I was fixin' to settle in, this feller, Liam Baxter, come to the door. I knew him, of course. He said he'd pay me well if he could leave his horse overnight in my shed. He give me this cartwheel, an' I heard him carin' for the animal. Somewhere he got a bait of timothy hay. I always admired folks that was good to animals."

Charley fished in a trouser pocket, put another cartwheel in the old man's hand, and started walking northward.

Morton was too stunned to call a thank you. It had been so long he couldn't remember when he'd made two silver, Yankee dollars in so short a time. Among his jumbled effects he had one thousand dollars — but in Confederate notes. Folks had said after the war the Yankee government would redeem them at face value. Lex Morton was still waiting.

What he had just been told made it possible for Charley to

understand one thing. Baxter had deliberately avoided the hotel last night. He had known the constable had a room there. Charley had been unable to get a good look at the bushwhacker, but he was satisfied now that the bushwhacker had got a good look at him. Quite possibly, either for just plain personal safety or because he thought Charley had recognized him, Liam Baxter had effectively avoided the constable.

Charley crossed the street and reached the far side several buildings south of Cork's water hole, when the stocky, corral-yard foreman, a genial, dark Mexican, stopped him, wearing a broad smile. "Someone stole a big flake of hay from our shed last night." The smile remained broad. "*Again*. That makes twice. I haven't told Mister Brennen. He acts like it's gold. We don't tell him unless it happens a lot."

Charley nodded as he looked past the Mexican's shoulder. "I'll look around," he said.

The Mexican shrugged. "Maybe someone needs hay for a milk cow. It's nothing, Mister Bent."

Charley went down through a dogtrot into the westside alley. The short-backed, muscled-up horse was dozing where his reins had been looped, but not made fast to a stud ring. Then Charley went back up to the plank walk, started north, but never reached the saloon. Liam Baxter came past the spindle doors, looking in the direction of the jailhouse. He didn't see the constable until Charley moved.

Baxter's holster was on the right side. He twisted a little, something Charley Bent had seen done many times and understood perfectly. Baxter had just yanked loose the six-gun's tie-down.

Charley addressed him without raising his voice. "Are you a better shot with that pistol than you were yesterday with a carbine?"

Baxter smiled without a shred of humor. "You need a faster

horse, Constable. After you left, I had a talk with Amelia."

"I told you to stay away from her."

The cold smile lingered. "You never saw the day you could tell me what to do. She's taken a shine to you, an' that's too bad for both of you. She wrote me out a deed to the ranch an' cattle."

Charley's gaze neither wavered nor blinked. Both men saw only each other. Otherwise, they might have noticed that the main street, which had tethered animals here and there, now contained no people.

Liam Baxter's back was to the spindle doors. Charley saw a flutter of movement there, but did not permit it to divert his attention. On the other hand, Liam Baxter, who was facing the street, might have seen the aproned man come to lean in the door of his harness shop. He had one hand behind his back.

Baxter broke the interlude of silence. "Nothin' you can do, Constable. I'll get the deed filed, an' she can have ten days to clear out."

Charley had no illusions about Liam Baxter, and he was too close. He hadn't expected the confrontation to occur as it had. He took down a shallow breath and allowed his right shoulder to drop a fraction, something Liam Baxter saw and understood.

The gunshots were close enough to sound almost as though they had been fired simultaneously, but almost was not good enough. The impact spun Charley. One leg buckled. As he was falling, he tried to twist for a second shot. This time there were three gunshots, and one sounded like a cannon.

Baxter had been hauling back his hammer for the killing shot. Cork Finney's sawed-off scatter-gun knocked Baxter off the plank walk. The second shot from the harness shop door-way wasn't necessary, but it did what the shotgun blast had not done — it punched a hole through Baxter's head from front to back. Death was instantaneous.

Cork dropped his scatter-gun and ran to help Charley stand. There was blood everywhere. Jed Ames came over with a six-gun shoved into the front of his mulehide apron.

They got Charley into the saloon, atop the bar, and Cork's reaction was typical for his vocation — he went for a bottle of whiskey. Jed Ames sliced the trouser leg from hip to ankle. He then told Cork to fetch a clean rag. He removed the constable's belt to wrap it around the wound and twist it until the bleeding stopped. The wound looked like raw meat.

Charley drank from the bottle Cork had forced into his hand, lay back, and closed his eyes. There was pain, but there was also numbness. Charley rose up for two more swallows from the bottle before he dropped it.

People appeared. Jed growled for them to stay out and to fetch Doc Reese. A few ran for the doctor, while others watched in silence from the doorway.

The graying medical man had to push and punch to get inside. He was carrying his black bag. He got close, put down the bag, and began examining the wound.

"Did it go clean through or is it still in there?" Jed asked.

"Clean through. Looks like a butchered beef, don't it? But the bone's not broke."

Jed gave ground, while he watched the physician work. Dr. Reese told Cork to fetch hot water and more clean rags. Then he told Jed to take the constable's gun belt off and pull up his shirt, which Jed did. Then the medical man went to work. He plunged both arms to the elbows in the hot water Cork brought and dried his arms on a clean cloth the saloonman provided before he moved up the bar.

"Charley, can you hear me?" the doctor asked. He fixed Cork with a fierce glare. "You fed him whiskey? Let me tell you somethin', you sot of an Irishman, when they're hurt, bad whiskey makes 'em bleed more. Ease up a tad on that belt, Jed. There's got to be blood going both ways, a little at a time. You stop it flowin' altogether, an' he'll likely lose the leg. Not that much, you idiot. Now tighten the belt again."

Although Leonard Reese, the Rock City doctor and also coroner, did enough business to get by, because of his acerbic disposition he was not very popular among those in the district unless they truly needed him. Right now he had taken control. He gave orders. He swore. He tried to make the constable talk to him, but Charley neither spoke nor any longer opened his eyes. His face was flushed, and he was sweating. The medical man sent Cork to his house to fetch a small, blue bottle.

When Cork returned, the doctor took the small, blue bottle, leaned on the bar, told Jed to force the constable's jaws open, and tipped in a bit of the liquid from it. Within moments Charley turned loose all over.

Cork said: "I'll be damned. He's asleep."

The physician threw a condescending look in Cork's. "He's got to be carried to his room at the hotel." He turned and called out names and several large, sturdy men came forward. Dr. Reese gave the orders. "Jed, you walk beside him an' keep that belt tight. The others of you, try not to let him sag."

One of the men was Andy Buck. He said: "It'll hurt real bad."

The doctor replied sharply: "He don't feel nothin' now but pleasant. He won't know no better until you get him a-bed up yonder." No one said another word, but he did. "Now quit talkin', an' carry him up there. Jed, mind you don't let the bleedin' start."

The procession from the saloon to the hotel was silent. Not until they all filed into the hotel, some even going into Charley's room to prepare the bed, did Ray Kemp appear. He knew what had happened, but, because he objected to so many people crowding the hallway and wasn't feeling all that well himself, he told them angrily to get the hell out and stay out.

Some left, but Andy Buck, Jed, and Cork Finney remained.

Kemp saw the blood and groaned.

Jed turned on him. "A man keeps you safe an' you moan because he leaks a little blood on your blankets."

Kemp's answer was quick. "A *little* blood! I've butchered hawgs that didn't bleed that much."

Jed took Kemp by the arm, pushed him out into the hallway, and closed the door.

The doctor got Charley settled, worked the belt so that circulation would not be entirely cut off, and told Cork to bring a chair so he could sit down.

As he did this, Cork asked a question. "What was in that bottle you give him?"

The physician turned. "Why? So's you can peddle it? You know what laudanum is?"

Cork shook his head absently.

"You drain that bottle, an' you'll drop dead. You still want to get some to peddle over your bar?"

Charley made a sighing sound.

The doctor asked: "Can you hear me, Charley?"

The constable mumbled something and opened his eyes. They did not seem to focus.

The doctor said: "One of you fetch some hot broth. Chicken's best, but beef'll do. *Go on! Get it!*"

After Andy Buck and Cork had gone, the physician leaned over the lawman and enunciated very clearly. "Constable, directly you'll come 'round, an', when you do, you're goin' to hurt. Do you understand me?"

Charley mumbled again, more distinctly this time. "Did I get him?"

The doctor pulled back slightly. "Someone did. I heard shootin', but wasn't there. Go back to sleep, if you can, because, directly now, I'll spoon some food into you, an' if you throw it up, I'll never be able to speak to you again. *Or her.*"

Charley didn't hear him, which was just as well. He had no idea gossip had spread so far.

Chapter Eighteen

A BUGGY RIDE

To close the wound the doctor looped cloth around it that had been dipped in hot water and cinched it fairly tightly. Because Jed was peering over his shoulder, he said: "As it dries, it'll get tighter." He finished with the bandaging and spoke again. "If it'd been six inches higher, it'd have busted his hip, an' only a miracle would have fixed that. As it is, it's going to take months to heal and he's going to have a sunken scar." He paused to look at Jed Ames. "Long as he keeps his breeches up, it won't show." He turned back to the bed before adding: "He'll have a limp the rest of his life. Who was the fellow who shot him?"

"A man from up north who was as fast with a gun as anyone I ever saw," Jed said. "Liam Baxter."

The physician nodded and began washing his hands and forearms. "I saw him briefly as I entered the saloon. Looked like he'd been hit by an explosion. Best be looking after his remains next."

Jed Ames did not comment.

Charley's first night was bad. Despite his best effort to ignore the occasional groans, Ray Kemp could hear them at the far end of the hotel. Jed Ames stayed with Charley through the night and well into the next day.

Late the following afternoon Amelia Thatcher arrived. Dr. Reese was at bedside when the ranch woman entered. He turned, rose, and gestured for Amelia to take the chair he had been occupying. His only comment was laconic. "The seat's already warm."

Charley was drenched with sweat. Amelia used a tiny handkerchief to absorb the perspiration around his eyes. She didn't speak. She was too shocked at his appearance to do that, but her concern was obvious and deep. She told Charley she had sent for a physician from Cheyenne. She also told him she wanted him moved to her main house at the ranch, and this brought an explosion from Dr. Reese.

"The only thing that's keepin' the bleedin' from startin' is the way he's bandaged. You take him out of here, an' so help me God he'll bleed to death before you go a mile."

Amelia did not look at the physician behind her when she said: "All right, but isn't there a nurse in Rock City? Someone who can mind him day and night?"

The doctor came up beside the chair and spoke softly to Amelia. "His friend, Jed Ames, was here over night with him. Lex Morton was here this morning. I told him to go home and get some rest when I came. I'd say Charley's doing all right."

Amelia sat a silent moment, gazing at the other. In appearance Dr. Reese did not inspire a lot of confidence. She said: "There are people who will stay with him day and night?"

The doctor, obviously somewhat irritated by her belated concern for his patient's well being, nodded curtly and replied: "There's been folks a-plenty up to now, and that isn't likely to change, ma'am. If you're of a mind to help yourself, you could go to the Emporium and fetch back some white, bleached muslin. It's got to be clean. And some lye soap, some grease, and some binding twine."

Jed and Amelia met on the porch. As he held the hotel door, he told her who he was and that he had returned to attend to Charley.

She said: "I've sent for a doctor."

Jed nodded at this and passed inside without another word.

Rock City wasn't quite in mourning, although there were those who were convinced the constable wouldn't pull through. They had the amount of dark stain on the plank walk to support this contention. Cork Finney did not allow pessimism in his saloon, but he worked so hard at being optimistic it rang hollow. In any case, there was no laughter and most of the townspeople were concerned and reserved.

That old adage that lawmen only have friends who are also lawmen did not apply in Rock City, and, meanwhile, winter arrived. It diverted attention to keeping stoves crackling as the snow came. The days remained gray and sunless for long periods, and Amelia finally abandoned driving to town every day and took a room at the hotel. It was room number 4, but she didn't learn who its previous inhabitant had been until much later.

Charley's progress was painstakingly slow. When the physician she had sent for finally arrived, he informed Amelia that Dr. Reese's treatment had been most effective, and, as long as the constable made no attempt to leave his bed, he would in all probability recover. The Cheyenne doctor gave Amelia a packet of white powder to be sprinkled on the wound each time the bandage was changed.

The only major difficulty Amelia encountered was when Christmas arrived, and townsmen trooped in to leave gaily wrapped bottles of whiskey, brandy, or some of Cork Finney's home brew, this last known to knock a man's socks off after two glassfuls. She developed a technique of interception that worked fairly well, except for Lex Morton and Ray Kemp. They sneaked in two bottles of pop skull from the kitchen when Amelia was not in Charley's room.

Winter in the high country was a time of foreshortened

vistas. Folks lived between the wood pile and the house. Sam Brennen's disposition was not improved when the stages had to plow through two feet of snow on the level and could not keep to their schedules. He visited Charley once, and that was less to sympathize than to state his firm conviction without a shred of evidence that Liam Baxter had been the highwayman. To this claim Charley responded: "He'll do until another one comes along." Sam departed, muttering to himself. Jed Ames and Amelia Thatcher formed a friendship. They took turns sitting with Charley.

As winter eventually yielded to spring, still with snow flurries and biting cold, there was runoff in all directions, and in windswept places new grass showed. Amelia told Charley one unseasonably warm day that she had to return to the ranch for a few days. It was something Charley understood and did not question. During her absence, he confided to Jed that, while he'd never been a marrying man, getting shot had altered several of his lifelong convictions, and the biggest one was that he had changed his mind about marriage.

When Amelia returned, she went to Charley's room and asked if he could sit on the edge of the bed. He could and did. She held out both hands. He gripped them and rose to his full height. She smiled. "I have to feed you up, Charley."

Holding both her hands, he smiled. "Nobody in this world I'd rather have feed me up, Amelia."

They stood an awkward moment before she released his hands, and he hitched unsteadily to the window. With his back to her, he said: "Once before, years back, I was down a-bed, an' the old granny who cared for me is the only person on earth who ever seen me in my underwear" — he turned very red — "except you."

She laughed and changed the subject. "I want you to do something for me."

He nodded. "Name it."

"I want to take you to the ranch. I'll feed you up, Charley."

They regarded one another over a silent moment before Charley replied: "It'd be an awful bother, Amelia. Here in town I get looked after like a baby."

"Charley . . . please?"

He smiled. "Yes'm. But I don't bend very good."

"You won't have to bend," she assured him. "I'll bring a wagon full of blankets."

"When?" he asked.

"Two weeks from today."

He nodded. "I'll be waitin', but I still think it's pilin' a lot of work on you, and I'll be beholden."

Amelia smiled while looking him straight in the eyes. "I want to, Charley."

After Amelia left, Jed came to visit. Charley told him what Amelia Thatcher had suggested. For a brief moment the harness maker's jaw set hard, but only for a moment, before he spoke. "Be real careful. Don't let 'er bump over rocks. Charley, she's one in a million, that woman is, for a damned fact. A body can't live as long as I have, without knowin' a few things. I think most likely the best thing that ever happened to you was your gettin' shot by that miserable bastard."

Charley had to ponder that after Jed's departure. He would have a limp for the remainder of his life. On the other hand, he was alive. It wasn't that he owed Amelia more than he could repay. Hell, he also owed Jed, Lex, and even Doc Reese. But Amelia Thatcher was — well, Jed had put it right — one in a million. He groped for the bottle hidden in the bedding and swallowed twice before hiding it again. He had pain and probably would have for months to come, but John Barleycorn helped.

Charley spent the next two weeks as restless as a bear cub in a bee tree. With the approval of the town council members, including Sam Brennen, Charley was able to appoint Jed Ames interim constable until he would be on his feet again. When the day to leave the hotel arrived, Lewis Boles angled the light, dray wagon close enough to the plank walk for the rims to grate. He had three Terwilliger riders on horseback along with him.

Amelia had ridden the full distance up front with the range boss. She hadn't said ten words until they were out front of the hotel. Then she gave orders.

People gathered to watch their constable being carried to the wagon and carefully placed atop an old ticking mattress and covered with heavy blankets. He raised an arm as the cavalcade headed out of Rock City.

There were puffy white clouds in the sky. The day was warm. Lewis Boles was a good teamster, but the best teamster on earth with miles of range country to traverse would not have been able to avoid every jolt. Amelia climbed into the wagon bed to hold one of Charley's hands. He was sweating like a stud horse, but he squeezed her hand and smiled.

The ranch house was ready. Charley had lost considerable weight, and yet it required all hands to get him inside the house and into bed. After the men filed out, Charley told Amelia her range boss was as good a driver as he'd ever known.

With evening approaching and the cold increasing, Amelia built two blazing fires, one in the parlor, the other in the kitchen. Charley was dog-tired. He would have slept but for the fragrance from the kitchen. He was ravenous without realizing it, until she brought a tray piled high with food. She propped him up, put the tray on his lap, and left the room.

When she had said she would feed him up, she had meant it. For almost fourteen days he ate like a starving wolf, and, while some of his strength returned, it was taking a long time, much longer than Charley, for one, had thought it would. Not until midsummer, in fact, could he walk gingerly and do simple chores. The range men did their best to ignore it when he'd have to sit down, or when the limp was most noticeable, which was usually, whether he would admit it to himself or not, when he got tired. Charley had never been an individual who surrendered to despondency, but as the warm weather wore along and his limitations improved only very slowly, he seemed to have no rise in spirit. He smiled less and talked less.

It was on a bright, cool, early morning when Amelia had the Crittenden buggy brought forth that Charley watched until Amelia came from the house, carrying a wicker hamper, and said she wanted to show him something. Then some of Charley's interest in life reappeared.

They left the yard, driving north on a slightly eastward course. There was little conversation. Charley had been on this drive enough times to know their destination.

The morning was perfect. The sky was a cloudless blue. There were birds in the grass, and occasionally they passed mammy cows with sassy, fat calves at their sides. Charley was not affected in the least when they passed the bush with its limp yellow ribbon, on their way into Cache Cañon.

Amelia stopped a hundred or so feet from the old, dilapidated log house. Charley dropped the tether weight and would have helped her with the picnic hamper, but she motioned for him to follow her. She went toward the closer west slope and then up it as far as one of those stone cairns. Charley was breathing hard when he reached her. Amelia faced southward, pointing in the direction of the other westside stone pile. "That one isn't even with this one," she said.

Charley nodded. He had noticed it the last time he had been here.

Amelia then pointed across the narrow cañon in the direction of the other two similar piles of rocks. She said: "The same thing, Charley. The farthest pile is not aligned with the second one."

He nodded again.

She turned and pointed once more. "Following those surveyed markers on a straight converging line, they would end up at the base of the cliff to the north."

Charley used a bandanna to mop off perspiration.

Amelia tugged at him. They descended to the cañon floor. As they walked, she began: "Whoever the surveyor was. . . ."

"His name was Ben Leathergood."

Amelia scarcely noticed the interruption. "He did not follow the map. Why? I would guess because he wanted to have his friends believe he knew what he was doing. And he *did* know. He knew he wasn't surveying according to the map."

They halted in front of the old cabin. Amelia asked if Charley was tired, got a negative head wag, and took him to the doorway. Inside, startled rats half as big as a house cat fled in all directions. When Charley entered, he said: "Someone's been here."

Amelia agreed. "I have. Can you lift that rotten floor plank?"

He lifted it and stood like stone.

Amelia said: "I didn't have to dig far. Whoever hid it must have been in a hurry."

She knelt, lifted two leather saddlebags out of a rotting wooden box, rocked back on her heels, and suggested: "Open them, Charley."

The saddlebags were filled with small leather pouches. Charley fetched out one of the leather pouches. It was curled and yielded easily when he opened it. The little pouch was full of gold dust and nuggets. He leaned on his heels, considering the cache.

Amelia smiled. "There is the cache of Cache Cañon and Cache Valley."

Charley tipped back his hat. "How'd you find it?"

"As I told you, that surveyor had to know where it was. My guess is that he had no intention of telling his partners about it. He led them to believe the cache was farther north, against that cliff. He must have to have known better."

Charley got to his feet, felt a twinge, and went to sit on some collapsed roof logs. He wagged his head. "If I hadn't seen this, I wouldn't have believed it. Hell, for years I've been telling folks there wasn't no cache. That it was someone's pipe dream. Amelia?"

She had stood up and was now dusting herself off. "Guess how much it's worth, Charley?"

His reply was candid. "I got no idea. That's a lot of gold. Amelia, you're a rich woman."

"Let's load it in the buggy," she proposed.

The difficulty in carrying the cache's contents was not entirely its weight. It was because the old box and the pouches which had rotted over the years broke apart when lifted. Charley filled his pockets. Amelia filled her skirt. They made three trips before Charley looked at the buggy springs. They were nearly arrow straight. As he climbed in, he told her to be careful of rocks or gullies because one good jolt would cause the springs to break.

She wondered aloud how long the cache had been buried under the floor of the old cabin. Charley, the lifelong lawman, wondered about the owner of the log house who had to have put it there.

They rode back with dusk settling. Amelia drove so slowly that, by the time they drew up in front of the ranch house, it was dark. Amelia told Charley she felt guilty, carrying the loot into the house in darkness.

He laughed at her. "I'm the law," he told her. "An' I'm helpin', which makes me just as guilty, except that there's no reason for guilt. I don't know anyone with a better claim to it. It's yours."

After they had unloaded the buggy, Charley got one of the men to lead the rig to the barn to unhitch it and care for the horses. Charley knew he was thoroughly exhausted. He stood in the cool night for a long moment before shaking his head. Then he started across to the now lighted ranch house.

Amelia had lamps burning as she worked in the kitchen. Charley leaned in the doorway, watching. As she handed him a glass of watered whiskey, he said: "I've been wonderin' lately how to ask you somethin', but after today I don't figure I'd ought to say it."

She stood directly in front of him when she replied: "Ask anyway."

"Well. . . ."

"Would it have made any difference, if we hadn't found the cache?"

"Yes, I expect so."

"Why?"

"Well, a town constable makes thirty dollars a month. I expect two people could live on that, but. . . ."

She interrupted. "Were you going to ask me to marry you?"

Charley looked over her head, let go a soundless sigh, and nodded without looking her in the eye.

Amelia told him to empty his glass.

He did.

Then she said: "When?"

Charley felt the color rising. "You're worth a lot of money. It ain't right for a man to marry a woman who's got more'n he has."

Amelia's steady gaze did not waver. "Charley, if that's what

204

you believe, for once do something you think is *wrong*." When he still seemed to be tongue-tied, she said: "All right, suppose a woman with money asked a man to marry her? Would that be wrong?"

Charley remained mute.

She said: "I'll ask *you* to marry *me*."

Charley smiled. So did she. Then they both laughed.

THE END

About the Author

Lauran Paine who, under his own name and various pseudonyms has written over nine hundred books, was born in Duluth, Minnesota, a descendant of the Revolutionary War patriot and author, Thomas Paine. His family moved to California when he was at an early age and his apprenticeship as a Western writer came about through the years he spent in the livestock trade, rodeos, and even motion pictures where he served as an extra because of his expert horsemanship in several films starring movie cowboy Johnny Mack Brown. In the late 1930s, Paine trapped wild horses in northern Arizona and even, for a time, worked as a professional farrier. Paine came to know the Old West through the eyes of many who had been born in the previous century and he learned that Western life had been very different from the way it was portrayed on the screen. "I knew men who had killed other men," he later recalled. "But they were the exceptions. Prior to and during the Depression, people were just too busy eking out an existence to indulge in Saturday-night brawls." He served in the U. S. Navy in the Second World War and began writing for Western pulp magazines following his discharge. It is interesting to note that all of his earliest novels (written under his own name and the pseudonym Mark Carrel) were published in the British market and he soon had as strong a following in that country as in the United States. Paine's Western fiction is characterized by strong plots, authenticity, an apparently effortless ability to construct situation and character, and a preference for building his stories upon a solid foundation of historical fact. ADOBE EMPIRE (1956), one of his best novels, is a fictionalized account of the last twenty years in the life of trader William Bent and, in an off-trail way, has a melancholy, bittersweet texture that is not easily forgotten. MOON PRAIRIE (1950), first published in the United States in 1994, is a memorable story set during the mountain man period of the frontier. In later novels he has shown that the special magic and power of his stories and characters have only matured along with his basic themes of changing times, changing attitudes, learning from experience, respecting nature, and the yearning for a simpler, more moderate way of life. He is presently at work on his next **Five Star Western**.